P9-DEU-078

THE STIRRUP BRAND

OTHER FIVE STAR WESTERNS
BY PETER DAWSON:

THE STIRRUP BRAND

A WESTERN STORY

PETER DAWSON

FIVE STAR

A part of Gale, Cengage Learning

GALE
CENGAGE Learning

Detroit • New York • San Francisco • New Haven, Conn • Waterville, Maine • London

GALE
CENGAGE Learning

Copyright © 2013 by David S. Glidden.
Five Star™ Publishing, a part of Gale, Cengage Learning.

ALL RIGHTS RESERVED.
This novel is a work of fiction. Names, characters, places and incidents are either the product of the author's imagination, or, if real, used fictitiously.

No part of this work covered by the copyright herein may be reproduced, transmitted, stored, or used in any form or by any means graphic, electronic, or mechanical, including but not limited to photocopying, recording, scanning, digitizing, taping, Web distribution, information networks, or information storage and retrieval systems, except as permitted under Section 107 or 108 of the 1976 United States Copyright Act, without the prior written permission of the publisher.

The publisher bears no responsibility for the quality of information provided through author or third-party Web sites and does not have any control over, nor assume any responsibility for, information contained in these sites. Providing these sites should not be construed as an endorsement or approval by the publisher of these organizations or of the positions they may take on various issues.

LIBRARY OF CONGRESS CATALOGING-IN-PUBLICATION DATA

Dawson, Peter, 1907–1957.
    The stirrup brand : a western story / by Peter Dawson. — First edition.
        pages ; cm.
    "Published in conjunction with Golden West Literary Agency."
    ISBN-13: 978-1-4328-2700-7 (hardcover)
    ISBN-10: 1-4328-2700-6 (hardcover)
    I. Title.
    PS3507.A848S753 2013
    813'.54'dc23   2013008087

First Edition. First Printing:July 2013.
Published in conjunction with Golden West Literary Agency.
Find us on Facebook– https://www.facebook.com/FiveStarCengage
Visit our website– http://www.gale.cengage.com/fivestar/
Contact Five Star™ Publishing at FiveStar@cengage.com

Printed in Mexico
1 2 3 4 5 6 7 17 16 15 14 13

ADDITIONAL COPYRIGHT INFORMATION

The Stirrup Brand first appeared as a four-part serial in *Short Stories* (7/49-10/49). Copyright © 1949 by Short Stories, Inc. Copyright © renewed 1977 Dorothy S. Ewing. Copyright © 2013 by David S. Glidden for restored material.

CHAPTER ONE

He stood on the coach's platform behind the tender, not minding the smoke and the jolting as the train ran in on Lodgepole past a scene that bridged the eight-year gap. The deepening dusk didn't let him see much. But it was enough to bring on a homesickness he hadn't known was in him. That hump on the far hill would be Sam Olds's dynamite bunker. Beyond, where the tall lodgepole pines thinned out, the skeletal chimney of Drury's lightning-fired stage station slid past, lonely and etched sharply against the deep azure above the broken horizon to the west. Then Carson's corrals laid a blur against the near darkness.

The brakes screeched and the coach was swaying violently as the first house lights came up out of the obscurity. He noticed that the slender spire of the courthouse was newly shingled, that a white-painted house stood on Ames's lot, vacant these many years. The faded lettering of the livery barn's sign with its backward "N" was the same, so was the brick-dust red of Bill Yount's saloon front.

Fred Vance picked up valise and saddle as the coach rolled in on the station's cinder ramp, an exceedingly tall man powerfully built across the shoulders but otherwise lean in every measurement. This quality was especially noticeable in his deeply tanned face. Its bony structure was quite pronounced and gave his wide-spaced blue eyes an intentness less noticeable when he smiled, which was often. His medium-brown hair was bleached at sides and back where his wide hat had let the sun hit it. His outfit was a shade better than the average cowpuncher's, being a black coat over a maroon flannel shirt, waist overalls just beginning to fade at the thighs, and a pair of soft well-fitting boots, polished. He wore a staghorn-handled .41 Colt in a holster, hanging low at his right thigh.

Loaded as he was, he stood nicely balanced against the train's jolting stop before swinging his high frame down the steps. He carried the saddle's weight easily, and as he stood there, looking back at figures moving to and fro in the light of the station lanterns, the expectancy and eagerness that had given his lean face a youthful cast gradually faded before a definite reserve. Finally he recognized one man's slim shape and his eyes lost their good-humored glint and became taciturn.

This man he had noticed with back turned, and in that moment Fred Vance's impulse was to walk on out across the siding and avoid this meeting. But then he thought—*Might as well get it over with.*—and sauntered back along the ramp. The other turned finally, saw him, and hurried his way.

There was no handshake—the saddle and valise helped there—yet the older man made a pretense at affability. "Damn, boy, you're big! Big as your father was. How are you?"

"Fine, Milt. You look the same." Commonplace as the greeting was, Vance was relieved to have it spoken. He'd been wondering what he'd say to Milt Hurd.

"Here, let me give you a hand." Hurd was only slightly ill at ease as he took the valise. And as they started around the station corner, Vance sighed gently, thankful for the moment being no more awkward than it was.

"Had your supper yet, Fred?"

"On *that* train?" Vance chuckled, looking obliquely down and finding it hard to believe that he topped his stepfather by nearly a head. He had always remembered Milt Hurd as being tall and

8

rowhead for a spell. The antelope are thick as ticks over there."

Vance was scarcely listening as his eye hungrily roamed the familiar dark street. Just then it came to him that no matter how far a man wanders, the ties of the early years are strongest. He'd like to stay on a few days and work this odd liking for the country out of his system.

They were passing Yount's lighted window and he caught himself about to suggest turning in there for a glass, remembering at the last moment his stepfather's weakness. Milt would need his wits about him if they were seeing Kirby. *The senator!* he thought wryly. He wasn't letting his mind dwell too long on Milt's betrayal of his mother's wishes in granting any lease. Instead, he was telling himself that times had changed, that she would have understood. Yet there was the nagging suspicion that this wasn't exactly so, that the change was in himself, in his no longer caring. It would be best for him to pull out tonight, to clear up this business and get out. He'd wanted to see Josh Hawks, the last of the old crew, even wanted to see Stirrup itself. But why probe at a nearly healed wound with any further reminders than he was having now? Stirrup was finished except as a source of small income. Its greatness that had steadily waned since the day his mother remarried was gone for good. And there was little point in blaming Milt Hurd. The man's drinking and his disregard for money were weaknesses that no longer mattered. The thing was done and Stirrup was only a magnificent picture hazed to near nothingness by the passage of the years.

"Your train was later than I'd thought." Hurd was hurrying now as they came abreast the hotel verandah and started up the steps. "Kirby'll be tearing his hair out."

"The hell with Kirby." Vance spoke mildly but meant it.

There were two brass-bound trunks standing by the steps and Vance dropped saddle and valise alongside them, noticing that a wagon with the legend *Transfer* painted along its sideboard waited at the street's edge. He heard the lobby door open and turned, thinking Hurd had gone in. But his stepfather was standing, hat in hand, holding the door wide for a tall and slender young woman with dark hair followed by two men lugging another trunk.

" 'Evening, Rita," Hurd said, his tone unctuous. "Looks like you're planning a long stay."

"We are, Milt. Better hurry on up. Dad's pacing the floor."

The girl came on out, glancing Vance's way as she passed. He was trying to see what this daughter of Kirby's was like, but the faint light showed him little more than the pale oval of her face and her dark, alive eyes on him.

He eased around the men with the trunk and followed Hurd into the lobby, and, as they started for the stairs, he said: "I'd forgotten Kirby had a daughter."

"Probably because Marguerite's younger than you. By six years as I remember it. She's just past twenty."

Now that his memory had been jogged, Vance could vaguely recall a gangling youngster in pigtails who had ridden a spotted pony to school. That was the only picture his mind's eye could summon of Jim Kirby's daughter as they crossed the lobby, deserted except for three men standing by the entrance to the bar. A low run of voices sounded from in there. As Hurd and Vance passed the counter by the foot of the stairs, they stopped again to step aside for a man coming down the steps, lugging a heavy suitcase. Once again Hurd spoke with that false affability Vance had noticed on the verandah. "Looks like he's clearing out for good, Bill."

"So it does." The man, shad-bellied and sober of face, took in Vance incuriously and went on.

There had been something familiar about him, and Vance,

following Hurd up the steps, asked: "Haven't I seen that one before?"

"More than likely. Bill Childers, the senator's wagon boss."

Of course. Only eight years ago Childers had been running a small bunch of cattle on a homestead over in the Rainbows, trying to get a start. He was older than Vance by a few years and Vance remembered him as being quiet and likable.

Upstairs they turned back toward the street and Hurd led the way along the uncarpeted hallway to the last door and knocked, sighing gustily. He was saying—"Now let's try not to ruffle the old. . . ."—when the opening of the door cut him short.

It was Jim Kirby who stood there. He was grayer, heavier perhaps, but beyond that hadn't changed at all. He was still as big a man as Vance had ever seen, so tall and solidly wide as almost to fill the doorway. His face was craggy, square, and his dark eyes piercing as they slid past Hurd and took in Vance.

"We thought you'd been shanghaied," he said in a deep, booming voice. "Come in, come in."

His brusqueness fitted him well, and, as Vance followed his stepfather on in past Kirby, he was feeling some of the resentment toward the man that had been so much a part of his upbringing. Just then he wondered as he never had before what the circumstances might now be had his father and Kirby stayed together as partners. They had come here as partners, bringing a herd of Texas longhorns, had together built the first sod-roofed cabin along the lush slope of the Wigwams to the north. A winter together had finished their partnership and the next spring they had gone their separate ways, two dominant personalities unable to get along under the same roof—or even on the same range, as it turned out. Over the twenty years of their differences John Vance had matched downright courage and shrewdness against big Jim Kirby's stubbornness and envy. In the end the elder Vance had won for Stirrup the heart of the rich graze below the foothills and Kirby had taken his pick of what was left, grudging Vance his holdings even after his death. It seemed that he was still keeping on with that fight.

Almost never did Fred Vance feel small in a man's presence. But now, as he turned to hang his hat on the rack by the door, following Hurd's example, the man's massiveness had that effect upon him. Kirby was lifting a hand to indicate two other men who had risen from chairs at the bay window overlooking the street, saying: "You remember Leonard Keely, Vance. And Tom Demmler."

Keely, the lawyer, was a spare, small man and Vance stepped across to shake hands with him as he said reservedly: "How are you, Vance?"

Then it was Tom Demmler, his square and ruddy face taking on a broad grin, who gave Vance the only genuine welcome of the evening. "Fred, you're a sight for sore eyes!"

"You, too, Tom." Vance could feel that Demmler's handclasp meant something and he was momentarily thankful for the presence of at least one man he could count on not to oppose him in what he sensed was coming.

Kirby was pushing the chairs out to make a wider circle, and, taking the one that had its back to the table lamp, he glanced pointedly at the clock on the mantelpiece, saying: "Sit, all of you. We've got exactly seventeen minutes before the train's due. Let's get this over with."

Keely, Demmler, and Hurd took chairs as Kirby was reaching to the inside pocket of his coat to bring out a sheaf of papers. He looked up at Vance. "Have a seat. Did Milt explain everything?"

"Nothing except that you want a lease." Vance hadn't taken a chair but was leaning against the corner of the table, hands in the pockets of his waist overalls. To remain standing seemed the simplest way of putting himself on an even footing with the senator.

Kirby eyed Hurd briefly in annoyance, then said: "Here's the arrangement. Demmler and I split the lease and between us pay two thousand a year. He gets the line camp at The Springs. I use the main layout. Briefly that's what this says." He slapped the papers across his open palm in a gesture of finality.

"Then there's the option, Jim." Keely inserted that quiet word as he leaned over the table to flick the ash from his cigar.

"Option?" Vance was taking a sack of tobacco from a coat pocket, about to build a smoke, when the door opened and he looked around. It was Kirby's daughter, and once again she was only a shape in the shadows he couldn't really see. "An option on what?"

"Stirrup. What else?" Kirby seemed annoyed at the closing of the door and looked around. "All right, Rita. I'm coming fast as I can."

"The things are on the way to the station, Dad."

"I know. I'll be along in a minute."

Kirby settled back in his chair to eye Vance enigmatically. "If we don't wait too long the layout's still worth something. Of course the house needs repair. I'll have to rebuild some sheds and the corrals. Then it'll cost something to grub out the thistles and string new wire at some weak spots. But. . . ."

"You've set a price?" Vance cut in.

Kirby's head had come up sharply. "Naturally."

"Mind telling me what it is?"

"My share would be ten thousand dollars, Tom's four."

A smile that was slow in coming broke across Vance's lean face. "This isn't a joke, is it?" he asked, glancing briefly at Hurd, and then back at Kirby again.

"Joke? Far from it." Kirby eyed Hurd disdainfully. "Just what is this, Milt? I thought you said you'd told him."

Tom Demmler shifted uneasily in his chair as Hurd lifted his bony shoulders, saying: "I had some idea of getting him here and thrashing it out." His look pleaded with Vance. "Fred, the place has gone faster than I could keep up with it. Last year it was a new roof for the barn, the year before repairing the foundations on the old part of the house. Your father had built them of rock and mud and they'd weathered so. . . ."

Fred Vance lifted a hand, waving him to silence. He was ignoring Hurd now, his attention on Kirby. "Fourteen thousand, is it? Let's see. That's something less than fifty cents the acre. Around three hundred fifty dollars the section. Has land come down that much around here since I pulled out?"

Kirby said nothing, only glared.

"How many rooms in the house?" Vance finished building his smoke and lit it, and Kirby gave a visible start at the sound of the match scraping the table's underside.

"Ten, I believe."

"A ten-room house, half log, half rock. How many miles of fence would you say? Sixty, seventy?" Vance laughed softly, though there was no amusement in him. "The day's long gone when you can steal land, Kirby."

The big man's hands gripped the arms of the chair. His face took on color and his dark eyes came afire with hostility. "You'll damn' well. . . ."

"Dad!"

Kirby's head came around at that quiet yet intent word. Looking across at Rita Kirby, Vance was once again disappointed at not being able to see her more clearly. She stood near the door, leaning against the wall looking at her father, or so the shadows made it seem.

Something in the quality of her mild reprimand now carried its weight with her parent, for Kirby's tone was more reasonable as he spoke again: "Look, Vance." He leaned forward in his chair, wagging a finger in emphasis. "I've had a crew in there for sixty days. There are upward of two hundred head of my beef inside your fence. A carpenter's at work on the house. And. . . ."

"And no lease."

Kirby stiffened and slowly came up out of the chair. It looked as if he were about to lunge at Vance. "Milt," he said, his regard not straying from Vance, "you promised that lease! Your signature's on it. Everything would be smooth as silk, you claimed. So I took you at your word and moved on in."

"Dad, we're missing the train." Not until the girl had spoken did any of them really notice the final note of a train's whistle moaning loudly and nearby.

Kirby listened and once again that sound came. "Rita, go down there and tell them to hold that train," he snapped.

"They won't. It's the express."

"Then listen, Vance." Kirby's impatience made him speak hoarsely. "I'm in there on a promised lease. I'm going to. . . ."

"You're in there on nothing but thin air, Kirby."

The senator visibly flinched and his jaw corded in anger. His glance went to Keely. "Len, I'll expect you to look after my rights."

But the lawyer only shook his head, looking at Vance: "It's not too good an offer, Fred. But not a bad one, either. You'll spend a lot fixing up the place. Have you got it to spend?"

"No."

"Then my advice is to get out while you can."

"Fred." Milt Hurd had to swallow before he could go on. "This is probably the last dealings we'll have with each other. I've had it in mind to go to the coast, to a lower country. So you won't have me on your hands after this is over. But it's my only chance to see my way clear. I can't go on here. I owe almost as much as my share if that option is taken up.

"You've always owed money." Vance hated having to insert this reminder. But he was seeing now that Stirrup mattered more than he had realized. "Give me a few weeks and I'll find an outfit to lease to. There must be a dozen cattle companies willing to go in there without the idea of buying. And at a better figure."

"Dad, we'd better be going," Rita inserted.

A rumbling sound came from the rear of the building and the floor trembled as the train rolled down the back alley. Jim Kirby came around the end of the table, standing within a stride of Vance now. He was fully erect, as though counting on his massive stature to carry his point.

"This is my last word. Will you sign?"

"No." Vance eased away from the edge of the table. "So start moving off the place."

For a moment he was expecting to be hit, was planning on exactly how he would roll with the blow and where he would throw his fist at that vast expanse of Kirby's coat front. Then all at once the tension broke. An enigmatic, almost smiling look eased the hardness from Kirby's craggy face and he swung to the door, taking his hat from the rack.

Rita Kirby stepped out into the hall and briefly her father stood regarding Vance in that same nearly smiling way. Then he was gone, the door closing behind him.

Milt Hurd's sigh struck across the stillness as Kirby's solid tread faded along the corridor. Then Len Keely broke the awkward silence. "Well, gentlemen, that's decided. Shall we go below and have a drink on it?"

"I could use one," Hurd said in a faraway voice.

"There's one thing more." Vance looked at Tom Demmler now, realizing his friend hadn't spoken once since the beginning of their talk. "We'll go ahead with your end of the lease, Tom. But without the option. That suit you?"

Demmler grinned relievedly and with open surprise. "Does it! I'm lucky to get anything. I've been the fifth wheel on this cart since the beginning."

"Understand, you don't get to buy. Not yet, at any rate."

"I get it. Sure."

"Then you can draw up the papers, Keely?"

The lawyer nodded. "They'll be ready by noon tomorrow. Only I hope you know what you're doing."

Milt Hurd came across and laid a hand on Vance's arm. His look was imploring as he said: "Take a second thought, Fred. Maybe there's a chance of your making a better deal. Then again maybe there isn't. This is two thousand dollars, a thousand apiece for us every year. I can get back on my feet again with that kind of money."

Vance looked down at him pityingly, without anger. "We won't go into my reasons for saying this, Milt, but I don't give a damn about your getting back on your feet. Not one damn!" And he turned away, going over to get his hat.

"I wish you didn't feel that way about it, Fred."

Vance merely shrugged, looking at the other two. "Ready?"

Demmler and Keely followed him out the door, Hurd not coming into the hallway until he had blown out the lamp and they were turning at the head of the stairs.

"Someone should have taken him in hand the day your mother passed away," Keely muttered as they went down the steps. And he added with a note of regret: "No one hates this worse than I do. I can remember some high times at Stirrup in John and Esther's day."

"You may see some again." There were vague stirrings in Vance's mind and he was wishing he could believe what he said.

They were halfway across the lobby and headed for the bar when the front door swung open abruptly and Jim Kirby and his daughter came in from the verandah. Kirby was carrying a suitcase and set it down when he saw them.

"Hope you're satisfied, Vance," he said aridly. "We missed it."

Vance shrugged. "There'll be another in the morning."

The blandness of his reply goaded Kirby into taking a step toward him. But then the girl laid a hand on her father's arm, saying quickly: "Please, Dad." And Kirby, his baleful glance holding Vance's for one more second, picked up his suitcase and made for the stairs.

Now Vance could see what Rita Kirby was like. It came as no surprise to find her looks striking, for he remembered her mother as being a handsome woman. The daughter had all of the mother's charm, and more. Yet the delicate pattern of her features was, strangely, the least interesting thing about the girl's beauty. It was the eyes, of a brown so dark they were almost black, that gave her face animation and a look of possessing a strong reserve of character. Those eyes met Vance's quite openly now; they were alive and full of an unmasked interest as she came across to them, to him.

"Has anyone warned you that Dad nurses his grudges, Mister Vance?" she asked, an amused glint in her eyes.

"No. But thanks for telling me. I'll remember."

She looked at Tom Demmler then, and there was a sudden warmth and gentleness in her expression as she asked: "You're staying in tonight, Tom?"

"Thought I would."

"Then could I see you in the morning?" She waited for his nod, and, giving Keely a brief smile, she said: "Good night, gentlemen." She followed her father.

Keely said—"Now that whiskey."—and he and Tom and Fred turned into the bar.

CHAPTER TWO

Some minutes later, after an awkward interval of casual talk, Keely bade them good night, and they ordered a second glass. Vance was suddenly remembering he hadn't eaten, so they took their drinks to the back counter where the apron presently set a plate of food before him. As he started eating, Tom Demmler eased away and with a broad smile, taking measure of his friend's high-built frame, drawled: "Brother, they ran to some outsizes when they put you together. But don't count on your size in this affair. Jim Kirby's big, too. Bigger."

"He's always been big, Tom."

Demmler laughed in that infectious way Vance had always liked. "And for as long as I've known him, always bucking a Vance. Well, here's to the Vance luck being what it always was." He emptied his glass.

Presently Vance wolfed down the last of the food and pushed the plate away. "Only one thing didn't add up tonight, Tom. You and Kirby together in the same room."

"Things change, man." Demmler's look was a guilty one. "But now that you've tripped us up, I can tell you he came to see me six months ago with the peace pipe. Because of you."

"What did I have to do with it?"

Demmler lifted his hands from the bar, let them fall again. "Everything. Kirby wanted this lease and knew you'd balk. Milt would've balked then, too. So Kirby wanted me to go to work on Milt. If I could persuade him, then maybe we could ease the

21

lease through without your kicking over the traces. I told Kirby you were sure to get red-headed but he convinced me it was worth a try."

Vance was eyeing his friend so soberly, so bleakly, that Demmler protested: "Sure, it looks like an underhanded trick now. But there was Stirrup going to hell. You were off somewhere and didn't give a damn about the place, and I figured I wouldn't be stepping on your toes. So I went ahead. Between us, Kirby and I were going to carve up the outfit. I played along with Milt till things were ripe. Only it turns out now they never were ripe."

"How did you play along with Milt?" Vance's voice was toneless.

"Used Kirby's money and paid off a few of his debts. Nursed him into thinking the senator didn't have horns and a tail."

"But throwing in with Kirby, Tom? I don't get it. Your old man would turn in his grave if he knew."

"So he would." Demmler was dead serious. "But remember what they say about beggars. If I can use that graze east of The Springs, I make a good living. If I don't, I'm just another man running a two-bit brand."

Vance was looking down at his hands folded on the counter before him. "Then there's the Kirby girl."

"Rita? What about her?"

"You tell me, Tom. Or don't, if you'd rather not."

"There's not much to tell . . . yet." Demmler picked up his glass and drained the last few drops from it, adding in an edgy voice: "Maybe I'm going against the blood lines, Fred, but I think I love her."

A slow expression of smiling wonder crossed Vance's face. "Forget the blood lines, you lucky devil!" He slapped Demmler on the shoulder. "Well, I'll be double damned! You can certainly pick 'em. Go after her, man!"

Demmler shook his head, looking embarrassed. "I haven't asked her yet. But one day I'm going to. Lola even likes her."

"Lola?" Vance guiltily remembered, wishing now he had thought in the beginning to ask about Tom's sister. "How is she? Married?"

Demmler's look was uneasy. "Yes. Or she was, rather. To a tramp that treated her like the dirt under his feet. She got rid of him, got a divorce."

"I see," Vance said quietly, understanding that there was something strange here. He was grave once more as, seeing that Demmler was about to add to what he had already said, he waited. But then abruptly Demmler glanced up along the bar, his look became disgusted, and he said: "Here we go again. Hard Luck Hurd himself." And hardly had he finished speaking when Milt Hurd stepped in alongside Vance.

"Like old times, eh?" Hurd said in a genial voice thickened by drink. He was obviously well under the influence. "Fred and Tom and Milt hoisting one together. It's my turn, boys." He tossed some silver to the counter and imperiously beckoned to the apron.

When the bottle was set before him, he was very solemn in pouring the drinks. He lifted his glass—"To the old days."—and downed the raw whiskey at a gulp. Then, as they drank theirs, he looked up at Vance with an eye squinted. "Let you in on something, Fred. A sure thing. Remember that stretch of alkali off by Turnbull's?"

Vance nodded.

"Well, sir, there's a man from back East that salted a patch out there with some powder. His own special formula, understand? Then he planted some timothy seed. Damn me if the stuff wasn't up finger-high in less than two weeks." He leaned closer, lowering his voice. "Now with three thousand between us, you and me, we can go to this jasper and get a deed for ten thousand acres along with enough powder to salt every bad patch in our piece. Barber Creek is off there and we could dam it up and have one of the. . . ."

Vance's shake of the head cut him off, and after a slight pause he asked querulously: "You don't think it'd work?"

"It might. But not for me, Milt. To begin with I don't have the money."

"But this is a sure thing. Get the money! Get it from Kirby and Tom here."

Again Vance moved his head negatively and now a subtle change rode through Milt Hurd. He stood straighter and his eyes became bright with anger. Quite suddenly, unexpectedly he snapped: "All right then. You can damn' well whistle for my John Henry on Tom's lease! I won't sign!"

Vance smiled in a way that lacked any trace of amusement and Hurd said sharply: "I resent this, Fred. It's become a point of honor with me that you don't trust me."

Vance's pale blue eyes were appraising the man coolly. He was aware that men to both sides of them had stopped talking and were watching, listening. When he spoke, it was to say ever so softly: "Milt, get away from me." He hesitated, then added: "I mean it. Now."

Milt Hurd opened his mouth to speak, closed it again. He seemed to shrink within himself in that moment as, deliberately, he turned and started out across the room.

He had taken three strides when he stopped abruptly and turned to them again. "Remember," he said loudly, "I don't sign that lease!" With that he wheeled around and made for the street doors.

Tom Demmler breathed a gusty sigh and shook his head, his look sharp with anger. "That poor damned sponge. Why can't they pickle him and put him away?" Vance said nothing and, noticing his preoccupation, Demmler quietly added: "I'll be going, Fred. If you're around in the morning, come on out to the place with me. Lola would skin me alive if I showed up without you."

"Then I'll see you out there, Tom."

"You're not staying here tonight?"

Vance shook his head. "No. Thought I'd drift on out and look the place over, stay there."

"Kirby's crew may not let you in."

"That's got me worried." Vance smiled meagerly. "Which reminds me. Where's Josh Hawks?"

"Josh?" Demmler chuckled. "No one's called him anything but plain Hawks for years. You might look at the cabin up Squaw. He's been trapping loafers and now and then bringing down a wild horse. You know Hawks, always on the prowl." His glance fell away, then lifted again. "Forgetting what Milt said, do you still feel the same about my lease?"

"Why not?"

"Well . . . you can't say I've played exactly square with you."

"You didn't know you'd be stepping on my toes. Forget it."

"You really mean that?"

"Sure. Now run along to bed."

"What if Milt won't sign?"

"He will, don't worry."

"Wish I could be as sure of that as you are." With that dry comment Demmler turned away, adding: "See you in the morning then."

Vance stood watching his friend until he was out of sight through the lobby doorway, grateful for this pleasant interval even though Hurd had spoiled the end of it. There was something so solid about Demmler—his square-built frame, his honesty, and straightforwardness—that Vance found himself genuinely pleased over the lease arrangement. Old Demmler had been a touchy, perpetually sour man and he was glad now that the son was having a chance to break out of his shabby heritage.

Milt Hurd was, of course, the main one to blame for the way things had gone tonight, for even having brought Vance down here, he was thinking. Yet Vance understood how Milt's sodden and desperate reasoning had driven him to do what he'd done. Kirby could hardly be expected not to take advantage to get his hands on something he'd wanted all these years, and Vance paid him a grudging respect in realizing this. Tom Demmler was the least guilty of anyone involved, for it was a human and natural thing to want to better himself.

Now Vance idly wondered what he would do about the balance of Stirrup—or all of it—if Milt Hurd refused to sign Tom's lease, which was a real possibility. In either case, should he try to lease to a cattle company? Or was it worth it to try to run cattle himself and slowly rebuild the outfit? It would be a different story than it had been with his father. A man couldn't go down into Texas any longer and gather up wild cattle or buy them for next to nothing. And Stirrup was top-heavy now with buildings and fences, corrals and line shacks that needed constant working and repair.

But the fact remained that, lease or no lease, he wasn't giving up the place. Nor was he letting Milt Hurd manage it from here on. It didn't matter that Esther Vance's will had made generous provision for Milt in making him co-owner until his death, after which the brand would go to her son or his heirs. Milt could do nothing to stop the outfit from being worked, and the more Vance thought about that the more the idea appealed to him. There was really nothing back in New Mexico he couldn't give up easily, nothing but a job and a few friends.

Finally, almost decided on how to go about this, he left the bar and walked out through the deserted lobby and onto the verandah. He stood there for several minutes, enjoying the coolness and the taste of a smoke he had rolled idly as he looked along the street. The walks were nearly deserted, though several times he glimpsed men on their way in and out of Bill Yount's saloon. One of these he was sure was Milt Hurd and his pity for the man deepened.

He remembered then that it was seven miles to Stirrup, that it was late, and that he'd better be traveling if he wanted much sleep tonight. His saddle and valise were still there by the railing, and, as he sauntered on over to get them, he was remembering Tom Demmler's guess that he might not be welcomed at Stirrup by Kirby's crew. That made him smile and he found himself looking forward to this possibility of a showdown with the senator.

He found the livery yard gate open as always, and his knock on the office door brought a sleepy hostler awake inside, calling to him to come on in. The man took his dollar and told him to take his pick of any animal but the sorrel and the black in the corral out back. While the hostler was getting back into his blankets, Vance took some things from the valise and, loosening the ground sheet encasing his bedroll, pushed them in and took out his bridle, and then retied the roll. The hostler sleepily had said he'd look after the valise.

Back in the corral beyond the long rank of carriage sheds and the barn, Vance had a hard time picking a horse because of the blackness. But after catching up the likeliest animal, a bay, he put on the bridle and led him over to the rail by the barn, where he had left his saddle. He was lifting the saddle when he caught a slur of sound hard to his left and looked around.

He had barely gone motionless when he saw a man's indistinct shape moving in on him. He heaved the saddle high and threw it, at once hearing the man's grunt of surprise as it collided with him. Then suddenly a driving weight slammed against his back and, as it brought him to his knees, a blow struck him alongside the head to lay a blaze of light before his eyes.

He tried to roll away, and the hard thrust of a boot grazed his shoulder. As he came to his knees, he saw this second one closing on him and dived at his legs. As they piled back against the side of the barn, his chest took punishment from a lifting knee. But then he was on his feet and slammed a hard blow in at the man's waist, throwing his weight forward to keep his opponent pinned there, lifting his head hard to catch the other in the chin. The man cried out hoarsely as his head hit the boards. Vance drew back and threw one vicious punch. Again the man's head banged the building. Only this time he didn't cry out, his shape going loose all at once and falling.

Vance sensed the first man coming at him now and wheeled a split second too late. He took a hard blow in the neck and, choking for breath, lifted hands to cover his face. Twice, a rock-hard fist numbed his right arm before he caught his breath and managed to stagger clear. He struck into the blackness, felt his blow glance off a shoulder. He swung again and this time connected solidly, feeling his knuckles bruise flesh.

Then as he swung a fast uppercut at the vague shape he missed and lurched off balance. An instant later came the sound of boots going away. His horse shied at something and a moment later the starlight let him see a thick shadow climbing the poles of the corral on the side of the alley.

He forgot that one then and walked over to where the other had fallen, reaching out with a boot to feel at the base of the wall. Nothing was there. He struck a match. It showed him only the bare, straw-littered ground. Then off at the edge of the light some object threw a deep shadow, and, turning over there, he found a hat lying in the dust. It was dirty gray, soiled through at the brim's inner edge and bent out of shape.

His neck was throbbing and he had the hat in hand as he

walked on back to get his saddle and lift it onto the horse. Then, about to toss the hat away, he abruptly changed his mind and folded it, pushing it in under one thong that held the blanket roll. He had little doubt as to where he could find the owner. It would be interesting to notice which of the senator's crew sported a new hat within the next few days. He wondered how to set about returning it.

Presently, as he led the horse on across and opened the alley gate, he was seeing how strong his luck had been. They'd had every intention of giving him a sound thrashing and now his impulse was to ride up the street to the hotel, rout Kirby out of bed, and tell him to have another try. But then a better idea came to him.

Half an hour later, when he came to the fork in the road leading north toward Stirrup, he kept straight on northeast into the hills.

CHAPTER THREE

Joshua Hawks was a light sleeper. Toward midnight he roused at the sound of hoof falls lilting faintly over the creek's steady racket. He had his reasons for being curious over the comings and goings of riders along this cañon so now he wasted little time in pulling on his boots, reaching the carbine down off the nails over the double bunk, and letting himself out of the shack's rear door. Below the wall corner a thicket of alder flanked the stream. He was out of sight in the shadows there when shortly a rider left the trail on the cañon's far side, waded his horse across the creek, and climbed the knoll toward the line shack.

Whoever this was reined in some fifty feet away and shouted: "Anyone home?"

Hawks kneeled there, frowning. That voice had a faintly familiar ring. But try as he would, he couldn't place it. He decided to wait.

The rider, a tall, wide shadow in the starlight, presently swung down from the saddle. But his shape told Hawks nothing except oddly to remind him of the way John Vance used to look, long ago.

"You there, Josh?"

It took that one word to bring a whoop of sheer amazement from the old wolfer. He broke through the thicket's edge with such a racket that Vance's horse shied and pulled at the reins. He came running up to Vance, dropped the Winchester, and took him by the arms, shaking him. "By God, it is! You lanky no-good maverick!"

Vance was grinning delightedly. "Maverick no longer, Josh. I'm home again."

"Not for good?"

"For good."

The old man was stunned, his expression one of disbelief. Then finally the full import of what Vance was saying struck home to him and he breathed wonderingly, almost prayerfully: "No."

Vance nodded. "Gospel truth, Josh. Let's sit ourselves down and I'll tell you about it."

Much later, after they had brewed some coffee and Vance had talked himself out, he leaned back in his chair and yawned. "Now it's your turn," he said, nodding to the shack's single window where a blanket hung over the glass. "Why that? And why were you waiting out there primed for trouble?"

"Just more of the same you been telling me, Fred."

"Kirby?"

Hawks nodded. "Last week they sent a man up here to tell me I had a week to move on out. This bird mentioned the lease and said from now on they'd do their own trapping. Maybe Bill Childers didn't have anything to do with it. I wouldn't know, but he's always been agreeable. Anyway, my time's up tomorrow. Today, that is."

Vance's glance ran around the small room, noting the pots and pans hung on nails over the stove, a stack of freshly cut wood, some of the wolfer's personal effects lying on an upended box below the window. "You'll have to hurry with your packing if you want to meet the deadline."

Josh Hawks only snorted and now Vance reached across to the bed for the gray hat, the one he had found in the livery yard. The wolfer had earlier identified it as belonging to Mel

West, one of Kirby's Box riders. Now Fred looked down at it speculatively, trying to decide something. Hawks was wondering what his thoughts might be but knowing better than to ask. This big, serious man, still awed him, was trying to convince himself that this was the same carefree sixteen-year-old who had pulled out of here eight years ago because he couldn't get along with his stepfather, the boy he had helped raise since the day he was old enough to sit a horse.

Shortly Vance looked across at him. "You sleepy, Josh?"

"Never was wider awake. Why?"

"Feel like a ride?"

Hawks lifted a hand to run a finger across his tobacco-yellowed mustaches, eyeing Vance quizzically as he tried to read meaning into the question. "Such as where?"

"Stirrup."

Slowly a light of eagerness came to the wolfer's eyes. "You mean what I think you do?"

Vince nodded, and, as though that was a signal he'd been waiting for, Hawks came to his feet. "Then let's be about it."

They rode away from the darkened cabin as soon as Hawks had climbed the slope and brought his horse down from the brush corral at the timber's edge. They wasted no time going down the cañon and, once out of it, cut southwest through the higher foothills. Twenty more minutes put them at the head of a long gentle slope with the timber falling away above and the deep grass swishing about their horses' fetlocks running downward as far as the eye could reach. Vance drew rein presently when a pinpointed light moved out from behind a lower hill's crest.

"Kirby mentioned how the place is run-down, Josh. Said it was grown up with thistles. But this looks the same."

"Not a thing's any different than it's always been." There was a dry edge to Hawks's voice. "Thistles, sure. But we've always

32

had 'em. Kirby'd like you to think the layout's done for."

Vance sat another long moment, looking toward that light, before abruptly nodding. "All right, I go in first. You swing off there and come in from the far side."

Hawks reined away at once and in half a minute was lost to Vance's sight as he went on. In five more minutes Vance could make out the dark patch of cottonwoods shading the house. The light was coming from the kitchen end of the crew quarters and he headed toward it, pulling the bay down to a soundless walk when he was perhaps two hundred yards away. He remembered the hat and reached around and got it, tucking it in his belt at the left side.

He went straight on and around to the front of the bunkhouse, stopping there, seeing now that the lamplight was coming from the kitchen window. He wasn't in any particular hurry getting out of the saddle; neither was he wasting any time. Dropping the reins, he walked to the door, pushed it open, and stepped inside, acting as though he belonged here.

For perhaps five seconds he stood there in the blackness, listening. He caught the heavy breathing of several men, heard one moaning softly, regularly. There was no way of telling what he'd bump into if he went farther into the room, so he took out a match and with his left hand wiped it alight on the seat of his pants. His other hand was resting on the handle of the Colt at his thigh as he moved to a table two strides to his left.

He had taken the chimney off the lamp and the wick was catching when a voice drowsily asked: "That you, Mel?"

He grunted an answer and carefully put the chimney back on the lamp, afterward facing toward the sound of a bed creaking. Then the light suddenly strengthened and he could make out the room's details.

Two double bunks were ranged along the back wall and there were singles on either side of the door. In the bed beyond the door a man wearing long underwear was pushed up onto an elbow, watching him. It was the man he had met at the foot of the hotel stairs back there in town tonight, Bill Childers.

They eyed each other soberly a long moment until Childers finally spoke a cautious word. "Well?"

Vance backed away from the lamp toward the bed on the other side of the door. Glancing briefly down, he saw that the man on it was asleep. He looked back at Childers then and reached down to a corner of the bed. He lifted it suddenly, turning it on its side. The man there rolled to the floor, thrashing in his blankets and cursing sleepily.

Childers was sitting up now. Vance pushed the overturned bed out toward the room's center as the man who had so rudely wakened came to his knees, wanting to know: "What the hell goes on here?"

There were only two others in the room, each in the lower of the double bunks. They were stirring now and Vance's look shifted between them and Childers and the other, who now came to his feet and backed toward Childers.

When he was sure that they were all well awake, Vance reached to his belt for the hat and tossed it across between the bunks. "Which one of you belongs to that?"

No one said a word.

"Go on, take it, West," Vance drawled. "How's your face?"

The man in the nearest double bunk unthinkingly lifted a hand to the left side of his face, quickly let it fall. And now Vance could see the swelling along this one's cheek bone and the heavy shadow of a bruise under that eye.

He heard a small sound outside now and instantly edged in behind the door. Shortly it swung back and Josh Hawks came in. He held a .30-30 loosely in one hand and Vance was the last man he saw as his glance ran round the room. He grinned wryly, nodding his approval. "Nothing out there."

Vance was watching Childers now. "Were you the other one?"

"Which other one?" Childers's voice was toneless.

"Two men jumped me at the livery in town tonight. West was one. Who was the other?"

Childers's puzzled glance swung across the room. "What's he trying to say, Mel? When did you get in?"

"Half hour ago."

"You heard what he said. Is there anything to it?" All at once Childers's look sharpened. "What's wrong with your face?"

When West made no reply, Childers snapped: "Talk, damn it! Who helped you jump Vance?"

West gave Vance a sullen look. "Red. He stayed in town."

"Why'd you do it?"

West gave a spare shrug. "We'd taken care of the boss' trunks and Red went up to see if the boss wanted anything else. He came back with this story of the lease bein' no good because of Vance. We had a few drinks. On the way up from Yount's we saw Vance headed for the stables. So we . . . well, who the hell said we couldn't rough him up a bit?"

Childers's look swung to Vance now, his eyes revealing little of his thoughts. It was obvious he wasn't going to add to what his crewman had said.

"Better get some men you can keep a halter on, Childers."

Vance was trying to prod the man into losing his temper. But Childers had a cooler head than he'd counted on and said mildly now: "Boys will be boys. But get to the point. What do you want?"

"I thought you knew. Your lease doesn't hold. You're moving out."

"I take orders from Jim Kirby, no one else."

"This time you're wrong. You're leaving. Now."

The man who had been rolled out of bed said—"You can't. . . ."—before the muzzle of Josh Hawks's carbine lifted sparely,

35

motioning him to silence.

"We can't what?" Josh asked. After a moment he hefted the Winchester once more. "Well, somebody move! Time's a-wasting. Pack your duds, boys. Stirrup's the wrong side of the fence for you from now on."

West and the man in the bunk next to him were the first to get out of their blankets. Then the one on his feet came across and began rummaging under the mattress lying on the floor. Childers sat watching for perhaps half a minute, then, his expression betraying nothing of his thoughts, he got out of bed and pulled on his pants. It was then that Vance crossed over to turn one of the chairs at the table around and sit with his arms folded over its back. The others were making a lot of noise as they gathered their things together, now and then speaking in sullen undertones.

All at once Vance saw the man standing in the doorway.

He didn't know how long he had been there, hadn't heard him approach. He simply looked across and saw him, noticing at once the gun hanging in his hand. And at about the same time Josh Hawks saw him and deliberately set the Winchester against the wall, his move warning Vance to be careful.

"Now what's going on, I wonder?" the newcomer drawled, startling the others even more than he had Vance and Hawks.

He moved on in until he could lean against the door frame. He was short-coupled with a barrel chest and bowed legs. He looked to be crowding forty with graying, mouse-colored hair. His eyes were a warm brown. He was mild-looking in every way, even with the drawn Colt. Yet now Vance abruptly caught the glint of lamplight from a nickeled star pinned to the pocket of his open vest and hastily revised his judgment of the newcomer's capabilities.

"Going somewhere, Bill?" The lawman was eyeing Childers.

Kirby's foreman tilted his head in Vance's direction. "He says we are, Sheriff."

The sheriff's lazy glance swung around. "Are you Fred Vance?"

Vance nodded.

"I'm Ben Sayers. What is this, an eviction?"

"You might call it that."

The lawman nodded sagely. "They told me something like this was liable to happen. You just get here?"

"Just." Vance was wondering why Sayers was talking chiefly to him.

The lawman lifted his Colt, looked down at it, let it drop to his side again. "They say you really told Kirby tonight."

Vance said nothing, and after several seconds the sheriff drawled: "And Milt Hurd."

There was still nothing to say, so Vance simply sat there, watching the man, judging him, knowing something more was to come. From what he had so far seen of this Sayers, he knew the man was to be respected.

The sheriff nodded now. "Yep, they say you told Milt off and sent him away from the bar there at the hotel with his tail between his legs. You didn't happen to follow him, did you?"

"No."

Sayers's brows lifted. "No? You didn't follow him on down to Bill Yount's and wait outside for him?"

"I didn't."

The sheriff gave a slow shake of the head. "Is that so? Because somebody did. Somebody with a gun that killed him as dead as he'll ever be. Vance, it looks like you're under arrest."

CHAPTER FOUR

The morning was bright and sunny and Rita decided to walk from the hotel to the station. There was, by some miracle, plenty of time. It was only 8:30 and the train wasn't due till 9:10. She wanted to stop on the way at Mrs. Parker's for a beaded bag the seamstress hadn't been able to finish until late last night but had promised to mail today. As it turned out, she met her on the way to the post office with the package.

Going on toward the station, she opened the package, took out the bag, and, after an amused glance at it, dropped it in the big leather purse she carried under her arm. Sight of that dainty and utterly feminine thing turned her thoughts to the trip East, to the opening of the house in Washington, and, honest as she always was with herself, she admitted now that she wasn't looking forward to a return to that life. She knew, without taking any pride in the realization, that she could long ago have had her pick of many of the men whose lives were bounded by the limited confines of the diplomatic and legislative circles; she knew also that none of them suited her with the everlasting emphasis they placed on social doings, their insincerity, and their lack of strong independence and self-sufficiency she had been brought up to expect in a man.

This train of thought shortly brought her face to face with her father's future and a wondering as to just what it might be. She frequently marveled at his insatiable ambition and now was one of those times when she asked herself just what limit he had set for himself. This trip home had been for the double purpose of oiling his political machine and directing Box's move onto Stirrup. Throwing cattle and a crew inside Stirrup's fence before the lease was an accomplished fact was typical of the way the senator did things. He was already picking his department heads in anticipation of this summer's announced resignation of the Secretary of the Interior, dead sure that he was to be named to the post.

Now that he had struck a snag in one of his bold moves she was almost hoping that he would strike one in the other. Lodge-pole range was her home and she had outgrown the excitement and curiosity over living anywhere else. Everything that meant anything to her was right here, bounded by the high line of peaks to the north and east, the tawny slopes to south and west.

Thinking of these things, she was oddly reminded of Fred Vance and became at once amused and halfway angry. It amused her to recall how quietly and stubbornly he had defied Jim Kirby in the hotel room last night; it irritated her to think that a man would dare stand in the way of something as reasonable as the Stirrup lease. The place was run-down; her father had, after all, gone in there on Milt Hurd's promise, and it seemed absurd for Vance to blow hot again the coals of an animosity the years had so completely cooled. He was a stubborn man.

Still, she was thinking as she turned from Main Street down the lane leading to the station, Vance was acting within his rights and what he intended doing with Stirrup was strictly his own affair. If her father and Tom had overstepped. . . . *Tom!* she thought guiltily, and stopped at once, remembering.

She started back for the street, ashamed of having forgotten him. Her every minute this morning had been crowded; a hasty breakfast, packing her overnight things again, then the nuisance of having the clerk bring her word that her father was delayed and that she would also have to see to getting his things to the station. No wonder she had forgotten telling Tom last night that she wanted to see him this morning, though now she couldn't recall exactly what had prompted her to go up to him and say what she had. All she recalled was a strong impulse of wanting a closer look at Fred Vance and of using Tom as an excuse for that.

Turning back onto the street now, she saw Tom on his way down the hotel steps. She was too far away to call out to him, and was relieved to see him go to the tie rail and mount his big bay, a magnificent animal with a chest blaze of white. He swung astride the bay and started her way and, as she waited there at the corner, she was feeling a glow of pride in thinking of him as the man of her choice.

He looked strong and solid in the saddle, his rather heavy frame in tune with the quiet strength she had discovered in him, and suddenly it struck her that, if she had one good reason for disliking Fred Vance, Tom Demmler was that reason. After all these years of hard, simple living that had been Tom's heritage from his father, he'd stumbled onto a rare opportunity in his share of the Stirrup lease. Vance had spoiled that chance for him and it gave Rita a turn now to contemplate the bitterness and galling disappointment this failure might work in him.

Now there stirred in her one of the few doubts she'd ever had as to the real basis of her affections for Tom Demmler. How much had sympathy, pity perhaps, influenced her in her liking for him? Hadn't both of these emotions played a real part in her defiance of her father in the beginning when he reminded her in his bigoted way that all Demmlers were a shady lot? Hadn't she set out to prove how wrong he was? Now that she had proved it, her father having gone so far as to make Tom his partner in the Stirrup lease, she was faintly annoyed at feeling so sorry for Tom because his luck had gone back on him.

But if this was any real doubt, it troubled her only momentarily, for shortly he saw her standing there and lifted a hand,
and she waved back to him. He used a touch of the spur as he
presently swung the white-blazed bay in to the walk's edge, and,
as he stepped aground, the smile she gave him was radiant, realizing as she was how much a part of her happiness he had
become lately.

"I was coming back, Tom. In all this rush I'd forgotten."

"Fact is I wasn't sure I'd get here myself." His good-natured
grin forgave her, though it was short-lived as his expression
turned serious. "They're all down there working Vance over. I
hated to leave."

"They're what? Who, Tom? What about Vance?"

He looked around and saw that her surprise was genuine.
"You didn't know Fred had been arrested?"

"Good heavens, no! Why?"

"Milt Hurd was shot last night. The senator certainly must
have known about it first thing this morning."

"Dad was gone before I was awake." Shock gave her voice a
low pitch. "They think Fred Vance did . . . killed Milt?"

"They think so. But he damn' well didn't, Rita!" Tom's look
was grim, furious. "I argued with Ben Sayers till I was blue in
the face. All he does is listen and nod and say . . . 'We'll see.'
The old fool. Next election we'll. . . ."

"Tom, you're defending Fred Vance?"

"Of course. Why shouldn't I?"

"After what he did last night?"

"After what he did? What he did was give me that lease."

"But I thought. . . ."

"He still won't take the senator's offer. My end's all right.
But, lease or no lease, Fred is all wool, Rita. Not a yard wide,
but two. They can't do this to him."

For several steps she was trying to get her thoughts straight,

41

and, when she next spoke, there was a slight edge to her voice. "Who would *they* be, Tom?"

"I honestly don't know. But someone's framed this killing on him, although he's got a weak leg to stand on."

"A weak leg? How?"

"He claims he left town around ten and rode up to that line shack on Squaw Creek where Hawks has been hanging out. Hawks swears Fred got there around midnight. Hurd was killed close to half past eleven. Which means Fred couldn't have done it."

"Then why was he arrested?"

Tom slapped the rein ends savagely across his open palm. "Who's going to believe Hawks? Sayers had heard about Fred and Milt having a set-to and about the lease being canceled. So he played a hunch and went straight out to Stirrup. Fred was there, moving the crew out, had just arrived. That made it look bad."

"Moving our men out of Stirrup?"

Tom nodded seriously. "A couple of them had jumped him here in town earlier, tried to give him a beating. It made him sore, so he went out there."

Rita was trying to take all this in and having a hard time of it. She said the first thing that came to mind. "Dad didn't know anything about the beating. That wouldn't be his way."

"No one blames Jim. The thing just happened and Fred wouldn't take it."

They were coming in on the wide platform alongside the express office now and Rita led the way across to the platform's edge. The worry on Tom's square face made her say gently: "If he's innocent, then it'll come out all right, Tom. Stop worrying."

"Wouldn't you try to help your best friend?"

"He's not your best friend." She was trying not to be

impatient with him. "You haven't laid eyes on him in years."

He shook his head and turned away, dropping the bay's reins and, with a visible effort, forcing himself to smile as he faced her again. "This is spoiling our good bye, Rita. I didn't want anything to spoil it."

"It's not going to be for long, Tom. Somehow, I'm going to talk Dad into spending the summer here. Washington's so hot you can't believe it."

He was hardly aware of what she was saying as he turned a thought over and over in his mind. She noticed that indrawn look and said: "Something else is worrying you."

He smiled guiltily. "Maybe it is, Rita."

"Anything you can tell me?"

His glance avoided hers now and he thrust his hands in pockets, then took them out again in a nervous gesture that made her laugh softly. Then, because she understood how shy he was at times, she hazarded a guess. "Is it about us, Tom? You and me?"

He nodded, his look grateful. "I was just wondering if I dared mention something."

She had helped him all she could, and now a sudden intuition in her reversed their positions and she was the one to be feeling an inexplicable embarrassment.

Tom must have sensed this, for when he spoke his words were halting, disconnected. "I was thinking that now . . . with the lease a sure bet, things are . . . well, different. If I have any luck next year, buy and sell right, then I. . . .

As he was speaking, Rita had noticed a rider coming along the lane and had gone tense, knowing an interruption was imminent and wanting Tom to finish before it came. But now he heard the horse walking up on them and turned, his words breaking off.

It was Bill Childers. He looked down at them and touched

his hat to Rita, reining his gelding to a stop close by. "Don't throw anything at me for the word I'm bringing, Rita. But it's another false alarm. The senator says you're to come back to the hotel. I'm to bring the trunks along."

"We're not taking the train? What's happened, Bill?"

"Vance."

"What about him?"

"Jim's had a talk with Keely. He's got a new notion on this lease and is staying on here. Must think he can do more good here than back East right now. Anyway, the trip's off."

Rita looked helplessly at Tom, shaking her head and saying in a small voice: "The least you can say for Dad is that he never lets things get tiresome. I'm sorry, Tom."

"I'm not. This is a break for me."

"What I meant was that I'm sorry you didn't get to finish what you were saying."

He was confused now by the presence of a listener and glanced briefly at Childers. "It can wait. It was only because you were leaving, Rita. Now there's plenty of time."

"Time for what?"

She knew what he had been about to say and he understood that and said gravely: "I want to be sure about this. Dead sure."

Childers cleared his throat, reminding them that they weren't alone. "You'll have to give me those tickets on the trunks."

Rita found the express checks in the pocket of her coat. As she handed them across, noticing how ill at ease Tom was, she wondered how long it would be before he again reached the point of asking her to marry him.

CHAPTER FIVE

Lodgepole's jail and sheriff's office made up one front corner of the county courthouse that sat in a small square dividing the town's residential and business areas. The building was of rock, shaded pleasantly by cottonwoods and poplars, and was given some distinction by an inset balcony across its second-story front and a high belfry, both of these being painted white and relieving the otherwise drab look of the structure.

The jail itself was as good as rock and steel and sturdy oak could make it. A steel grating ran its width two thirds of the way between outer and inner walls, this space in turn divided by another series of bars to form two cells. Set in the rock wall of the narrow aisle fronting the cells was an oak door with a small barred opening in its face at head height. The jail was gloomy, there being only one small opening near the ceiling, on the outer wall, this also barred by inch-thick steel.

Now, as the lock on the door grated and the heavy panel swung open, the strong sunlight slanting in from the office window made Fred Vance squint. He eased up off the near cell's creaky cot and eyed Ben Sayers's thick-middled shape as it moved through the opening.

"Finished eating?" the lawman wanted to know.

Fred nodded down at the heavy dishes and cup and saucer stacked neatly on the floor at the front of his cell. "Long ago. Any news?"

Sayers shook his head, sorting through his keys and finally

selecting one that he inserted in the lock of the steel grating. "Not much. The doc found the bullet and brought it in. She's out of a Forty-One."

That was Ben Sayers's way, leaving it like that. He had Fred's gun and he knew it was a .41. Now, as he turned the lock, he lifted his chin, indicating that Fred should move farther back. Then, when Fred did, he opened the door and grunted as he stooped to pick up the dishes. Although he didn't seem to move fast, it wasn't five seconds between the two turns of the key that left the cell as he had found it.

"So it was a Forty-One. How many like that would you say there are around town, Sheriff?"

"Must be all of fifty. More maybe."

"Then it doesn't prove a thing."

The lawman shrugged. "It's evidence."

"Look, Sheriff. If you want evidence, send a man out there to the layout and have him look above in the meadow for sign. A good tracker could follow that hired horse all the way up to the cabin along Squaw."

"Maybe do that myself when I find the time."

"When you find the time." Fred breathed a long sigh, trying to be patient. Then he remembered something and, as the lawman was going back into the office, said: "If you see Tom Demmler around, tell him to stop in."

Sayers nodded and swung the door shut.

Stretching out on the cot again and staring into the gloom, Fred reached absent-mindedly to his shirt pocket for tobacco. But then he caught himself and brought his hand away empty. His mouth tasted as stale as his thinking had gone. There wasn't any use in his trying to make sense of anything. Milt Hurd was dead, killed by a bullet that could easily have been fired by his Colt; there were witnesses to his argument with Milt in the hotel bar last night; there was the solid motive of Milt's death having made him sole owner of Stirrup; no one would listen to Josh Hawks because they knew he'd lie his head off for the son of the best friend he'd ever had. This was one sweet mess.

Just to have something rational to think about, Fred turned his mind to the problem of winding up his affairs down in New Mexico. He'd have to write Strickland and tell him to get a new man to run his layout. He owed something like $30 to the general store in Magdalena. He'd ask Strickland to sell his three horses, pay that bill, and send on the rest of the money. *Nothing else?* he asked himself when he'd sorted that out. No, there was nothing. He could break off from that life without a single regret, not one. His roots down there hadn't struck so deep after all.

Try as he would, he couldn't help wondering about Milt's dying. Perhaps it was a quirk in his thinking that had made him discard from the beginning any idea of Jim Kirby's being behind the shooting. Kirby had every reason to resent Milt's deception in regard to the lease. But to use a bullet on a man, to shoot without warning as the killer had done, wasn't Kirby's way. It followed, then, that Milt had made another enemy. He hadn't been able to think who this might be, nor had Sayers. "Milt was just too confounded harmless for anyone to waste time hating him," was how the lawman had put it.

The time dragged heavily, and presently Fred dozed, then slept, waking to see the late afternoon light dimming in the small window at the top of the back wall. He sat up and ran a hand through his hair, then rolled a smoke because of nothing else to do. There was a pail of water by the cell's door and after another minute he went across there and, leaning over, emptied the dipper over his head. The water was lukewarm but it made him wider awake.

He was dropping the dipper back in the pail when the lock on the outer door rattled.

It was Tom Demmler. Sayers, before he shut the door on Tom, said: "Give it a kick when you want out."

Tom stood in the narrow aisle after the door had closed and shook his head. "He's a trusting old boy. Took my Forty-Five and my knife. Felt of my pockets. Maybe he thinks I was bringing in a hacksaw."

Fred had unknotted his neckpiece and was drying his face with it. "Anything new, Tom?"

"Nothing good."

"Josh around?"

"Haven't seen him. But Kirby is. He's called off his trip. I'd give a dollar to know what he's up to."

"I'll take your dollar. He's going to stay on Stirrup. Which is why I wanted to see you." As Tom stared at him soberly, Fred turned to toss the wet bandanna to the cot, asking: "Any ideas on where I could pick up two or three good men to work for me?"

"I'll look around. They say Walt Stevens is on the loose. He'd be one possibility."

"I said good men."

Tom frowned. "What's wrong with Walt?"

"He's no hardcase."

Abruptly a look of understanding crossed Tom's face and he said softly: "Do you want that kind?"

Fred nodded. "The tougher the better."

"To take over the layout from Kirby?"

Again Fred nodded. "To take it and keep it."

The other sighed deeply. "That's a big order, friend. Unless you want me to ride up Summit way and have a look."

Summit was a dreary, half-deserted cluster of buildings near the top of the pass road almost at timberline, the haunt of rustlers and men who did their traveling at night. Remembering that, Fred said: "As good a place as any to start."

"What can you pay?"

"I'll leave that up to you. But I want men, Tom. That kind. The sooner the better."

"Suppose I find you some. What do they do? Wait around till you're out of here?"

"That's about all they can do. But I won't be here long." Demmler's slow nod and his grave look made Fred add: "Once you've done the hiring, you're out of this. You can tell Josh about it. Between the two of us we'll manage."

"I'll go up there tonight. Anything else?"

Fred thought for a moment. "If you can find some flowers, send some to the funeral for me. No card or anything like that."

"They're burying Milt tomorrow morning at ten. He was a Baptist, you know."

Fred grinned wryly. "Maybe that's why he took so easy to the liquids."

"Maybe so." Tom wasn't amused. "You're sure about this other, about wanting to tie into Kirby?"

"Why shouldn't I be?"

"I only wanted to know. Because this puts me on the spot."

Fred frowned uncomfortably. "Because of Kirby's daughter?"

"That's it," Tom admitted with a rueful smile.

"You're to stay clear of this. I'll look out for myself."

"Unh-uh. You've tossed some luck my way, so I back your play, whatever it is."

Fred's glance softened. "We'll see. Get going now and let me know how you make out."

Demmler turned and kicked at the door and presently, as it opened, he gave his last word: "Got a couple of ideas already. I'll let you know."

Out in the office he took his .45 Colt and clasp knife from the desk. Behind him, Sayers said: "Y'know, he don't strike me as being the kind to hide in an alley and let a man have it in the back."

"Then turn him loose, Ben."

The sheriff chuckled. "I'm not that convinced."

Tom sauntered on out into the courthouse hallway, spoke to a man coming from the office opposite, and went on down the steps to the street. He looked at his watch, saw that it was 5:20, and decided to eat. Forty minutes later he left town on the bay horse and headed up the pass road.

CHAPTER SIX

It was eighteen miles to Summit. Tom Demmler took nearly four hours riding the distance, not wanting to get there too early. When he did turn into the widening of the road that ran between the pines and saw the cobalt shadows of the ramshackle buildings ahead, he rode straight for a particular one and came aground in front of it by a broken tie rail. His bay was well trained so he dropped the reins, stepped around the rail, and crossed the rotten plank walk.

A stranger to the settlement would never have bothered pushing open the door in the building's boarded-up front the way Tom did. Once the door swung back, a feeble rectangle of lamplight flooded briefly out across the walk. Tom went in, closing the door quietly behind him.

Shortly he came out of the building with a man shorter than he and much slighter. This one's face made a narrow pale pattern in the starlight, and, as they talked, he assumed a spraddle-legged stance, hands on hips, the dead stub of a wheat-straw cigarette hanging from the corner of his mouth.

He listened to all that Demmler had to say and afterward asked: "What's in it for me?"

"Nothing but wages as far as Vance is concerned, Jeff."

Smiling crookedly, Jeff Spane drawled: "You wouldn't come all this way just to offer me sixty a month."

"No. You've played this game before. Follow your nose."

"So that's it," Spane said softly, speculatively. "How many

51

head would you say Kirby's run in there?"

"Around a couple hundred he claims."

The smaller man whistled softly, obviously interested now. "How many of us would it take to swing it?"

"Three on the inside is all Vance wants. You know best about the other end. Only Vance isn't to know about that."

Spane deliberated a moment, then asked: "Beginning when?"

"Right away. Move in on Childers tomorrow night, if you can."

Spane's head came up. "Bill Childers?" His narrow face shaped a wry grin and he said feelingly: "The more I hear of this the better it sounds. But why tomorrow if Vance is locked up?"

"Why wait? Vance may change his mind."

"It'll take some hustling to make it that soon."

"Don't you want it?"

"Hell, yes, I want it."

"Then take your bunch in there and play it rough." Tom ambled on out to the bay. "As rough as you can without burning any powder. Get men you can keep in line."

"I'll keep 'em in line," Spane drawled.

"Another thing. You'll probably be taking your orders from Hawks soon. Know him?"

"The wolfer? I know him." Spane's tone was dry, biting.

Tom swung astride the bay and was turning away when Spane said worriedly: "This Kirby now. He plays for keeps. This is a bigger game than the others you've asked me to sit in on, friend."

Tom brought his horse to a stand, looking around at the man. "Losing your nerve, Jeff?"

Spane visibly stiffened. "Don't be so damn' touchy. I'll be there."

Tom came back down the mountain faster than he had climbed it and shortly after midnight turned the bay into his

Cross D corral.

Sometimes he would look the place over with a critical, disdainful eye, and tonight this was the way he saw it, the four-room cabin with the sway-back porch he hadn't bothered fixing, the sideless barn with the meadow hay spilling down over the roof of the wagon shed, the downward narrow bay of the small meadow crowded by the pines. He hated the timber most because it had become a symbol of the throttling dreariness of this high country that didn't give a man room enough to move cattle around in, that brought hard winters and short summers and nothing but a struggle to make ends meet.

That was his mood as he went into the cabin's main room. He had lit a lamp and thrown his hat and coat onto a chair when he heard Lola moving around in her room. He thought bitterly: *Not tonight!*

This thought was purely defensive and was remotely associated with his contrary annoyance over the neatness and bright color he saw all about him in here. This room was like the rest of the house, not including his own which he had pretty well succeeded in keeping Lola away from except for the making of the bed. She had the same passion for orderliness as for making ends meet no matter how few the dollars might be. The buckskin-upholstered settee was typical of her ingenuity; she had patched all four worn corners exactly alike, lacing them with rawhide so that the patches looked as though they belonged. She used calico flour sacking for curtain material, and her party dress was the one their mother had been married in, made over, of course.

Sometimes a feeling of guilt and a realization of his shortcomings would keep Tom busy for a day or two at the endless chores he'd neglected about the layout. But those times were rare and didn't last. Normally he did only what had to be done and let the rest go.

So he made the best of it when presently his sister's door opened and she came into the room. She was holding a bright blue wrapper about her slender, small body and she smiled him a welcome as she reached up and brushed back a loose strand of her lustrous red hair. She looked relaxed and sleepy, her face placid, and he told himself—*She's damned good-looking, anyway.*—as she came over and kissed him on the cheek.

"You're late, Thomas. Can I make you some coffee?"

"No. Think I'll turn right in."

"I looked for you last night and stayed up with that new catalogue until almost one. They show a pump in there for only twelve dollars. Do you think you could get me one for the kitchen?"

"I'll get to it one of these days, Sis," he said wearily.

All at once a thought took the sleepy look from her eyes. "You've seen Fred." And at his nod she asked: "How is he?"

"Fine. Still the same. Bigger. He asked about you."

She went to the settee and sat with a leg tucked under her, patting the cushion beside her. "Come on, tell me about him."

He wanted nothing so much as to go to bed, but, knowing her, he came across and sat, watching her. "To begin with, they've locked him up," he said bluntly. And at her look of amazement he began telling her about last night and today, Lola now and then interrupting with a question.

When he had finished, she was staring at him speculatively, in a way that made him ask: "Now what's wrong?"

"Nothing, Tom. The lease is the best thing that's ever happened to us. And I'm glad someone's helping Fred."

She had a way of putting a double meaning to her words and now he sensed she was doing that and it annoyed him. "You're asking why it has to be me? You're saying I was wrong in hiring Spane for him?"

"You got him what he asked for. No, I didn't say you were

54

wrong." She spoke quietly and with what sounded like a trace of irony.

"Then you're thinking of Rita," he said defensively.

Her brows lifted and he wasn't at all sure she wasn't smiling inwardly. "You're putting words in my mouth, Tom."

He came suddenly up off the settee and paced between it and the door, hands thrust in pockets and his lips set in a firm, thin line. She was watching him with that same disquieting look.

"What's Jim Kirby ever done for me?" he asked all at once.

"Nothing, Tom. Nothing except include you in the lease."

"But who cinched it, fed Milt his booze, and thawed him down?"

"You did."

He was staring at her coldly, his temper really on edge now. "Do I just forget what Kirby did to the old man because of Rita?"

She was a long moment giving her reply, and as it came there was no change in the probing glance she had fixed on him. "We all have our problems, Tom. That's yours. Mine was Ralph."

"Ralph was no good. He was another Milt Hurd."

"So I left him." She was calm, unruffled in that way so typical of her.

"Then you want me to call it off with Rita? I don't dare step on the senator's toes? Hell, girl, I'm only helping a friend."

"Who is fighting Rita's father? You or Fred?"

In a gesture of exasperation he picked up his hat and tossed it to the table so that it skidded off and dropped to the floor. Then he was looking at her again, speaking in a normal tone for a change. "Why must you always take it upon yourself to be my conscience, Lola?"

"You've done all the talking, Tom. I've simply listened."

He was getting just so far, exactly as far with her as he usually did and now he saw that he would only be the loser in continuing this pointless argument. He shook his head wearily and sauntered over to the door of his room, stopping there to look back at her again. "If you're up early, wake me. I'll have to go in and tell Fred how I've fixed things."

"In the morning I have to go into town. Why don't I tell him? There's plenty you could be doing here."

"So there is," he said dryly, resenting her reminder of the countless things he'd neglected. "All right, I'll sleep late."

When he had slammed his door, Lola sat staring after him in that same speculative way. And presently she was asking herself: *I wonder what it is he really wants?* She thought she knew, and the knowing wasn't a pleasant thing to think about.

CHAPTER SEVEN

Lola drove the buckboard in to the foot of Lodgepole's main street just short of noon the next day and decided to do her errands before stopping at the courthouse. She was looking forward to seeing Fred Vance, for her memories of him were pleasant, even a little exciting. But it had become her habit to be deliberate about anything concerning her emotions—Ralph had taught her that—so she decided to finish her errands first and began at the dry-goods store and went from there to the restaurant to eat lunch.

Sidney Connover found her there and sat at her table a few minutes, presently asking if she would enjoy going with him to the Corlett's cabin raising. He was one of the few young men around who had seemingly forgiven her for her unfortunate marriage. He would one day take over his father's hardware business and ranch, and would be quite a catch. Still, after smiling at him in a way that might or might not have meant anything, Lola told him: "You'll have to let me see how things work out, Sidney. I'd have to stay in town all night."

He seemed grateful for even that much encouragement, and, when he had gone, she paid for her meal, and then walked on down to the feed mill to see what sort of a trade they would make on wheat for some baled meadow hay off the ranch. Tom should be doing this, but there was an unspoken agreement between brother and sister that she was the best bargainer. So she used her feminine wiles and some of her charm on old

Harry Wilson and by the time she left he had not only agreed to the trade at her terms but had mentioned the church supper next Wednesday night. As a deacon he reflected the town's feeling and she was comforted by that; they were forgiving her.

It was past 3:00 when she brought the last of the bundles out from the Emporium to the buckboard and then walked over to the courthouse. Now that the moment for meeting Fred was at hand, she had a queer feeling of uncertainty, almost of shame over what he might think of her. Did he know about Ralph? How much had Tom told him? But as she opened the door to Ben Sayers's office, her pride bolstered her and her uneasiness quieted.

The room was empty, a thin curl of smoke from a burned-down cigar in a can lid on the desk telling her of recent occupancy. A feeling of keen disappointment struck through her.

She was turning to go out when she noticed the small door inset in the face of the jail entrance. It was closed. She went across there, twisted its latch, and found that it came open. Set in the head-high rectangular opening was a steel grating, beyond it blackness.

"Fred?" she called hesitantly.

She heard a sound from in there. "Who is it?"

"Lola. Lola Demmler."

"Of course. Now I know you." His deep-toned voice sounded pleased, eager, as he added: "Get Sayers to let you in."

"He's not here. Before he comes back, there's something Tom wanted me to tell you, Fred. He's arranged everything with a man by the name of Jeff Spane. Spane will be at Stirrup tonight with his men."

"Tonight?" Fred asked. Then he decided it really didn't matter that Tom had changed the plan, that his men would go in without him, and added quickly: "Fine. Is this Spane a good man, Lola?"

"You didn't want a good man, did you?" She smiled knowingly, reminding him how grown-up, how wise she had been even in her girlhood. "Spane has a bad reputation. Does that answer your question?"

He chuckled. "Sounds like he's exactly what I need," he drawled, their talk touching only the surface of his thoughts as he stared across, studying the face framed by the lighted opening in the jail door. Lola made a pleasing picture there, the sunlight behind her giving her face a gentle, perfect outline and highlighting her coppery hair. And from some remote corner of his memory there came alive a quickening interest in this sister of Tom Demmler's. "This was something I was forced to do, Lola," he told her.

"I understand. Perfectly."

"I'll keep Tom out of it. Don't worry about that."

"I won't, Fred." A look of tenderness came to her now as she went on: "You've given us something we never dared hope for."

"Forget it. We old-timers have to stick together." Fred gave way to an impulse then, saying in a half-joking way his memory told him she'd understand: "You're prettier than ever, Lola. What's the matter with the men around . . . ?"

As he caught himself, knowing he had said the wrong thing, Lola told him quietly: "There was a man, Fred. Something went wrong."

"It must have been his fault," he said lamely.

Just then the awkward moment was broken as the hallway door opened. Lola turned from the door to find Ben Sayers entering the office. When he saw her, surprise took the slackness from his face.

"Well, hello, Red!" he said cordially, eyeing the opening in the jail door. He reached for his keys. "Here, I'll let you in."

"There's no need, Ben. I'm going to have to leave or it'll be dark before I'm home." She turned to the opening again. "Good bye, Fred. Next time in I'll bring some cookies. Or a cake."

"Next time you won't find me here," came Fred's answer.

"He'll be here," Sayers grumbled in mock severity. "You just bring along that cake."

She said good bye to Fred again, and Sayers opened the door and came out into the hall with her.

"Is it really as serious as it looks for him, Ben?"

The sheriff sighed gustily. "At times the case against him looks mighty thin. Then I add it all up and it holds water. I just don't know. Kirby's clapped another warrant on him and you know the senator."

"Yes, I know him." She forced a smile. "Well, I have to be going. I was serious about bringing him that cake. Tell him so."

"I will."

After she had gone, Ben Sayers went into the office and made himself comfortable in his swivel chair. There was a Cheyenne paper he hadn't finished reading. He had barely settled down to it when someone came into the office.

Lowering the paper, he saw big Jim Kirby standing there, a cigar jutting from his mouth at an upward angle. And, since he was quite aware politically, Sayers at once came to his feet.

He was about to say hello when Kirby cut him short. "Ben, I want to talk with Vance. Out here where I can get a good look at him."

"Well, now. I don't know." Sayers didn't much like the proposal but didn't want to offend Kirby in any way. "You'd be responsible, of course. It's your warrant we've got on him now."

"Then bring him out here."

By the time Sayers had opened the jail doors and Fred was coming into the room, Kirby had taken the swivel chair. "Sit down, Vance," he ordered gruffly.

Instead of doing that, Fred crossed the room and leaned back against the broad, hip-high sill of the open window. Sayers looked momentarily alarmed but decided to keep his mouth shut.

Kirby was scowling at Vance. "Leave us alone, Ben."

The sheriff's eyes opened a trifle wider. Then with a shrug he went to the door. "Remember what I said. He's your look-out."

"I'll remember."

After the lawman had gone, Kirby drew deeply on his cigar, and, as Fred regarded him impassively, he reached to his vest pocket to take out another. "Smoke?" he asked, offering it. But Fred only shook his head. So Kirby laid the cigar on the desk, remembering he hadn't offered Ben one.

The shaft of sunlight shining around Fred made a heavy fog of the smoke and only now did Kirby realize that he had been outmaneuvered, sitting as he was facing the light. This was what put an edge of irritation in his voice as he abruptly announced: "Vance, I'm not here to argue whether you did or didn't kill Milt. The court can decide that. My private opinion is that it's good riddance. Milt Hurd was as no-account as any man I've ever had dealings with. I hope you'll be different."

When Fred still had nothing to say, Kirby became uneasy. You couldn't argue with a man unless he talked. Or maybe the time hadn't arrived for arguing. Kirby decided to make it arrive.

"You own all of Stirrup now, Vance. Your say goes. We've made a bad start, you and me. But I take it you've got some of your father's brains. Use them now on this lease. If you'll. . . ."

"No, Kirby. You don't get a lease."

"Now wait!" Kirby lifted a hand. "Wait'll I've had my say. Maybe it's the price you object to. All right, we'll talk price."

Fred coughed, waving a hand against the smoke. "It's not price," he said, and, half turning, lifted the lower sash of the window higher.

Kirby took careful notice of that move as he reached over and put his cigar on the edge of the desk. "Then what is it?"

"The layout's not for lease. Or for sale. It never was."

"You might get three thousand dollars, even thirty-five hundred a year from a cattle company. Suppose we begin at thirty-five hundred."

"That's your offer?"

Kirby nodded.

Fred shook his head. "No dice."

"Four thousand then."

This time Fred didn't say anything, only shook his head.

Kirby's face reddened and he burst out: "Vance, you're a fool!"

The faintest trace of a smile came to Fred's eyes. He shifted so that his side was to the window now and lifted one boot to the sill, folding his arms over his bended knee as he sat and leaned back against the frame.

Kirby watched that in a knowing way. "Just try to make a break for it," he said softly. "Go on, try. Fall out through the screen. You might make it around the corner before I could get my gun out. Maybe you could make the back street and get on a horse, get clean away. Go on, try it."

That hint of a smile on Fred's face became real now, for it was as though Kirby had read his mind. "Maybe I will," he drawled. "But why should you want me to?"

"So I can hunt you down. So I can get rid of you."

"So you can get Stirrup, you mean. You've always wanted it. You thought you had it until last night."

"I'll still get it."

"How? Not by killing me."

"I'll get it through the courts."

Fred laughed.

"You think I won't?" Kirby's eyes went narrow-lidded now. "Today, not four hours ago, I turned that lease with Milt's signature over to Keely so we could bring suit against you."

"No court around here is going to uphold that lease."

"Probably not. So I'll take it to a higher court."

"They'll turn it down."

Kirby was smiling now in a pitying way. "Son, do you know how long a man can keep a case in the courts if he wants? Years. Three, five, seven years, who knows? I'm delaying every possible way. You can't last that long. You'll go broke and I'll win my case. Unless, of course"—and he paused significantly—"they hang you for murder and save me the trouble."

"You don't even have a case against me, Kirby."

"Which brings up another point," the senator said smoothly. "I'm in no hurry to bring you to trial. I'd just as soon they postponed it till the next term of court. That's sixty days from now. Then, when they do get around to trying you, Keely can stall. It might take two or three weeks. All this time I'm on Stirrup and you're here. There's not a blessed thing you can do about it."

Fred thought that over and shortly nodded. "So I'd better take the other way."

"Which way's that?"

"The way you just said. Get out of here."

Kirby smiled. "Try it."

"Or," Fred drawled blandly, "there's still another. . . ."

He lunged then, throwing himself sideways and out. He was falling against the screen before Kirby, intent on his words, started reaching under his coat for the gun at his armpit. Fred looked back over his shoulder as the screen gave way and saw how close it was to be.

He landed on hands and knees after the four-foot drop to the ground. He heard Kirby's bellow—"Ben!"—and threw himself in a diving roll for the corner of the building. Then, as his shoulder hit the ground, Kirby's gun blasted at the window and a spray of brick dust from the building's foundation corner hit him in the face.

He lunged to his feet and ran as hard as he could the length of the building, hearing shouts from the front as he made for the walk at the edge of the back street only twenty feet away. Two horses were at the tie rail beyond the walk. The sorrel was the biggest, so he chose that one. He ducked under the rail, jerked loose the reins, and swung up into the saddle, turning out into the street.

He was bent low over the sorrel's neck and the animal was at a full run when the explosion of a single shot echoed after him. That bullet kicked up a geyser of dust thirty feet behind the sorrel.

At the edge of town he cut wide of the road and headed fast up the near hill slope into the pines.

CHAPTER EIGHT

They had been waiting at the edge of the timber above Stirrup for almost an hour, their horses tied well back out of sight, and now as the night crowded out the last of the twilight and the stars came agleam, Jeff Spane said: "Let's move."

They mounted and started down across the long meadow toward the distant black shadow of the cottonwoods, Spane taking his time, riding straight for the winking lights of the windows of the crew's quarters. After several minutes they could see the faint glow of another light under the trees and, as they rode down behind the corral, Spane said: "Chuck, go look the house over." The man to his right started cutting obliquely away as Spane added: "Remember, no gun play."

They had talked it over pretty thoroughly up in the timber while they waited for the darkness, and now the third man, Byars, swung to the far side of the corral as Spane kept straight on. Byars knew his way about the place and would go in through the cook's lean-to, bringing the cook along if there was one.

All this careful preparation was unnecessary as it turned out. A man sauntered to the bunkhouse door and glanced idly into the night as Spane was coming quietly aground out front. But then Spane saw him turn back into the room and sit on the end bench of the table, and, as Spane was walking toward the door, the man reached for a platter and helped himself to some meat. They were just beginning the evening meal after working late. This was fine. They would all be there.

65

Spane simply stepped into the doorway with his Colt in hand and lined it at the table. "Don't anyone move," he drawled, and it was over. Except for Bill Childers.

When he heard that voice, Childers's head lifted. He laid down knife and fork, staring at Spane over the length of the table. There were three men sitting with him, counting Zinn, the carpenter, and each of them looked from Spane to Childers now.

He said mildly: "No one ever had to use a gun to get a meal off Box, Spane. Sit down."

He heard a sound coming from the kitchen behind him then and turned. Byars was roughly pushing the cook in through the door.

Childers knew now that this was real trouble. He was even more sure of it several seconds later when Chuck came in the door behind Spane, saying: "No one up there, Jeff. So we got 'em all."

Spane nodded, still looking at Box's wagon boss. "I heard you boys were on the way out, Bill. How come you haven't left yet?"

The cook made his mistake just then, thinking they'd forgotten him. He lunged for the kitchen door, and Byars swung sharply, striking with his gun. The blow caught the cook on the side of the head and his heavy frame went slack, crumpling to the floor.

Childers saw the last of it and was rising up off the bench when Spane called sharply—"I wouldn't, Bill!"—to turn him rigid as he was wheeling around. "Better go over 'em."

Spane had no sooner spoken than Chuck came across and started circling the table. He took Ed Foster's Navy Colt, searched Zinn for a weapon he never carried, found nothing on Red Durns, the one who had so far neither moved nor spoken. And he was careful coming in behind Childers to lift the .44

from his thigh. The cook was moaning softly now, a line of scarlet glistening from his scalp down to the floor.

"OK, boys." Spane's tone was amused. "Vance says you leave. So out you go. All but Bill."

None of them moved. Childers abruptly asked: "How would you know what Fred Vance says, Spane?"

"Didn't I tell you? I work for him now."

Childers's expression was one of utter contempt. "Scum like you working for Vance?" He shook his head.

Spane's face darkened. He said tonelessly: "You wait, Bill. Just wait." Then he came in behind Foster, lifted a boot, planted it in the man's middle, and shoved him toward the door. "Out."

They obeyed then, Zinn reaching his hat off his bunk, Foster and Red going out bareheaded. Chuck, their guns slung by the trigger guards in his left hand, was following when Spane told him: "Take 'em as far as the fence."

When Spane and Childers and Byars were alone, Spane nodded to the cook. "Drag him out and have the others take him along."

Byars got a hold on the unconscious man and pulled him out through the kitchen, Childers watching with a growing feeling of uneasiness and dread. He had never had any illusions as to the breed of man Jeff Spane was; he had none now. Finally his feelings crowded him into asking: "Now what?"

"You'll see. We've been a long time getting around to this."

Childers wanted to get it over with, whatever it was to be. He came around the table until he stood in front of Spane. His pale eyes showed his contempt, his loathing of the man. The door to the kitchen creaked shut now and Spane's glance went that way briefly. Then he was drawling: "You know what to do, Byars."

Childers heard the man closing in behind him. His thought of moving came a fraction of a second too late. As his body swayed forward with the thought, Byars's arms closed around him. He thrashed and kicked, but the other was strong and had spread his boots wide.

Deliberately Spane thrust his Colt into its scabbard. Then just as deliberately he drew back his right fist and threw it at Bill Childers's face.

The blow was a glancing one on the mouth, nearly a miss. And as Childers licked the blood from his lips, he said quietly: "Make a good job of it, Spane. Because if you don't, you're dead!"

"That was for the time you invited me away from Yount's poker layout in town, Bill. Remember? You'd never sat with a rustler, you said." Spane's laugh was brittle. "Now this'll be for those three days you kept me locked up while you followed that bunch of steers you never found."

He was smiling wickedly as he feinted with his left. Childers ducked straight into his hard right. Childers's head snapped back, and before it had rocked down Spane hit him again, and still again, standing crouched and his sloping shoulders rounded, grunting as he moved. His thin face was patterned with viciousness and his eyes showed a gloating as he swung once more on the helpless Box man he had so long feared and hated.

Childers was feeling nothing now, the last hard blow on the jaw hinge having almost knocked him out. He was weak, sagging against Byars's hold, and, when Byars dropped him suddenly, he fell face down, his smashed nose hitting the floor hard to bring on a new wave of pain.

That pain was what brought him around, cleared his senses so that he could make out voices. One was Spane's, the other a familiar one but not belonging there. He got a forearm under his face finally and propped his head up and opened his eyes.

Byars's boots were planted there close to his face and he could see the Colt that hung in the man's hand. Beyond, Spane was some eight feet away and facing the door. And in the doorway stood a high shape Childers had trouble recognizing because the lamplight didn't reach quite that far. But finally he knew that it was Fred Vance.

The next moment Vance was coming into the room, Spane backing slowly away from him and his hand warily lifting toward the gun at his thigh. Childers was noticing that Vance was unarmed as Vance looked down at him, saying tonelessly: "No one said you were to beat anyone half to death."

"Play it rough, Demmler said. That's what I'm doing."

Bill Childers noticed the cold angry way Vance's glance lifted to Spane now. "You take orders from me, Spane. Get this man onto a bed and do something for him."

"Like hell," Spane drawled. "This is something I've had coming to me for years. So keep out of it." He backed another step toward Childers. "Byars, keep your iron on him while I finish this. We don't even know if he is this Vance."

He turned then and reached down to take Childers by the hair and roughly lift his head. As the room rocked before Childers's eyes, he saw Fred Vance lazily reach up to push his wide hat onto the back of his head in a baffled, angry way. Childers was thinking groggily—*All he can do is stand there and watch.*—when suddenly Vance whipped off his hat and threw it at the lamp.

In that second before the lamp crashed to its side, Spane sensed something and let go his hold on Childers, wheeling around. As the room went all at once pitch black, Childers used every ounce of his feeble strength striking out at Byars's lifting gun arm.

Childers's fist struck Byars's arm a glancing blow at the instant the man's .45 laid its deafening blast along the room. That hard-reaching thrust carried Childers forward and into Spane's legs and Spane fell, cartwheeling backward over the

Box foreman as the thud of Byars's dropped gun sounded. There came the quick scuffling of boots, the solid strike of a fist, and the sound of labored breathing close ahead as Childers dragged his weight around and threw himself chest down on Spane.

Somehow he managed to get a hold, to pin Spane's arms to his sides, and, as they rolled out across the floor, Childers heard steps pounding toward the door. A moment later there came the crunch of boots against the gravelly soil outside, and he knew that Byars had gone.

Spane was cursing, struggling in panic, and finally lifted a knee hard into Childers's groin. The pain paralyzed the Box man an instant and Spane tore free, got to his knees, and lunged away.

Childers lay there, trying to get his breath, gagging at the strong taint of coal oil in the air and looking toward Spane silhouetted against the doorway. He saw Vance's high shape suddenly appear framed against the starlit opening, moving in on Spane. Vance must have sensed his quarry standing close then, for he planted his legs wide and threw a vicious swinging blow that caught Spane on the arm and staggered him across so that he was briefly targeted before the door. Now that he could see his man, Vance stabbed out with his left. Spane took the blow in the chest and staggered out of Childers's sight toward the table. One of the benches there fell heavily on its side and there came the sound of the table skidding and banging against the bunks. Vance lunged into that pitch blackness, and a moment later Spane grunted in pain. Childers could hear Vance's labored, gusty breathing, and the sound of several thudding blows. Then abruptly Spane's thin shape moved into sight again.

He was running, trying to make the door. He was almost to it when the small bench used at the near end of the table sailed out of the darkness to catch him squarely in the small of the back. He cried out hoarsely in agony and sprawled headlong through the door. Childers saw him scramble to his feet and hurriedly limp away.

A moment later Vance's voice came out of the darkness, halting, labored. "You all right, Bill?"

Childers had a hard time speaking and mumbled: "Go . . . after him."

"Let him go," Vance drawled. "We'll sit tight till they've cleared out."

His step sounded close by, and Childers wanted to speak, to urge him to finish what he'd started, but the effort seemed too great, so Childers lay as he was, shortly sensing that Vance was groping around in the dark trying to locate him.

"Just take it easy," Vance said from alongside. "Listen."

Childers caught the rapid hoof beats of a pair of horses, and, although it galled him to think Spane was getting away, he felt a contrary relief as the excitement drained out of him.

"They won't be back." Vance went to the door and closed it and over the next half minute Childers could hear him moving between the windows by the bunks. Suddenly a match's flare laid a wan, flickering light across the room, and Childers could see Vance standing there, looking down at him.

Blankets were hung over the windows. The heavy table sat crookedly, tilted against the double bunks along the inside wall. Close by an overturned chair, a glass-littered puddle of coal oil stained the floor, and now Vance stepped over there to pick up the unbroken base of the lamp. There was still some oil in it and with a second match he lit the wick, righted the table, and set the lamp on it.

Just then Childers saw the cedar handle of Byars's Colt sticking out above Vance's belt and the thought of how thoroughly the big man had turned the tables on Spane struck him as funny and he tried to laugh. But instead of laughing, he caught his breath and choked back a cry against the pain in his mouth.

Something was wrong with his jaw, his tongue was caught on a tooth, half bitten through, and his low whimper brought Vance across and kneeling beside him.

"Better let me get you to bed, fella."

Childers was remembering now what they had done to him. He sat up, and, as Vance tried to help, he pushed him away. With a vast effort he got to his feet and started for the door.

"Where to?" Vance drawled.

"Home."

"Better wait till morning."

Childers shook his head so violently that it unsteadied him and he lurched into the wall.

"Let's fix up your face first," Vance said.

"No."

"Can you stay on your hull?"

Childers nodded as he tried to pull the door open. Behind him Vance blew out the smoking lamp, then came to the door and opened it. He held Childers's arm as they went out. Childers trudged over to the bench by the wall, got the dipper from the water bucket there, and drank. The water's chill eased the pain of his mouth, and he emptied the dipper slowly, relishing it, feeling his numbed senses clearing a little.

Presently they started on again, heading for the corral. Halfway there, Childers asked: "What're you coming along for?"

"To see you get there."

Childers stopped, facing Vance in sudden anger. "I can. . . ." He had said that much before his hand lifted to his hurt mouth. Then he continued with a quick intake of breath: "I can make it on my own."

Vance smiled meagerly. "Sure you can. But I want to go along. It's a nice night for a ride."

Childers's anger was short-lived. He was feeling oddly grateful at the prospect of company over this long ride and a contrary friendliness toward this man whose very name had before now aroused nothing but dislike in him. There was something he wanted to say to Vance, but he couldn't quite get straight what it was. So now he simply turned away and stumbled on across toward the barn lot.

He was clumsy with the saddle, and Vance helped. Since Childers's animal was alone in the corral, they left the gate open. Vance walked on up to get his horse from the deep shadows between wagon shed and blacksmith shanty. While he was gone, Childers tried to get his boot into the stirrup and climb into the saddle. But his horse kept shying away and he wasn't quick enough to manage it. Then Vance was back again and held the bridle, and Childers finally managed to lift his weight up and go belly down across the leather, and then drag his leg over and sit straight. He felt foolish and his weakness put his temper on edge.

When they started out to the head of the lane, Childers had to concentrate on keeping his balance. He doggedly gripped the horn and held on, and it wasn't until they were nearing the rock outcropping at the foot of the pasture fence that he was steady enough to realize Vance had his reins and was leading his animal. That irritated him and very deliberately he fell forward against his horse's neck, snatched at the reins, and managed somehow to push himself straight again.

Vance looked quickly around and slowed until they were riding abreast. "Better?" he asked.

"Nothing's wrong," Childers muttered.

"Sure there isn't. You're doing fine."

Childers gauged those words sensitively, trying to find mockery or sympathy in them. But there was none. Vance had spoken matter-of-factly.

That started a strange and troubled train of thought in Childers on which he concentrated so intently he was barely aware of the passage of time or the miles they covered. Once his absorption broke before the surprised awareness that they were traveling the trail below Turkey Hill. How they had come that far without his realizing it he neither knew nor cared, and presently he lapsed once more into his pain-wracked reverie that had to do with Spane, Vance, Stirrup, and the contradictions this night had brought. His thoughts of Vance were quite searching and surprisingly logical; there were things about the man he'd had no way of understanding until now.

Long afterward—how long it was, Childers had no way of knowing—Vance drawled abruptly: "Someone's coming up behind us." Childers roused to the realization that they were riding the town road close below Box. He caught rapid hoof echoes from behind him along the road and turned to look back there, seeing two bright orange spots of light down the road, guessing from the rhythm of the sound that it would be a team pulling a light rig of some kind.

Then Vance was saying: "It's likely some of your folks. Keep straight on." And before the other could speak, he had reined away in the darkness.

Vance, as he rode clear of the road, pulled in and sat, watching the buggy come up out of the shadows. The team was at a fast trot and the buggy was close to Childers before the lamps brought him into sight. The driver pulled in quickly and said something unintelligible at this distance, and then abruptly another voice, a woman's, cried out in alarm.

"Is it really Bill?" Vance heard her ask.

It took Vance but a moment to be sure of that voice. He had heard it two nights ago in the lobby of the hotel. It was Rita Kirby.

Only later was he to wonder at the chance he took then. At the time it seemed the logical thing that he should draw Byers's .45, lift rein, and start in on the buggy. By that time Rita and the man with her were standing in the road closely beside Childers's horse. They were talking, although he couldn't distinguish their words.

Rita was the first to hear him coming and turned to face him, her look startled. Then the man's head swung quickly toward Vance, and he took a step out from Bill's horse, his right hand starting toward the handle of a gun at his belt. Abruptly he saw Vance's Colt lined at him and his hands lifted slowly, warily, to the level of his shoulders.

"Vance." Rita breathed in a barely audible voice as Fred came well into the light of the buggy lamps and swung down out of the saddle.

He walked over to her companion and lifted a short-barreled weapon from the man's belt. And then enough of the girl's surprise left her to let her ask: "What are you doing here?"

Vance was tossing the Box range man's gun across into the buggy now as Childers chuckled, saying: "Get him to tell you about it. We had one sweet scrap."

Rita's glance hadn't strayed from Vance and in her bewilderment she said: "But they're looking for you. How does it happen . . . ?"

"Looking for Vance?" Childers wanted to know. He was sitting, hunched forward tiredly in the saddle, and he spoke with an obvious effort.

"He broke jail this afternoon," the girl's companion put in tonelessly.

With a pointed glance at Rita, Vance came in beside Childers's stirrup then, and reached up to take a hold on the Box man's arm, drawling: "Time to get down, Bill."

Childers pulled his arm free, saying querulously: "I stay where I am."

"Why, when you can take it easy?" Vance nodded to the other Box man, adding: "A little help, friend." Then, before Childers could draw away again, he reached up and took a hold on his belt and pulled hard.

Childers came out of the saddle heavily, trying to push them away. Once he was aground, he would have fallen but for Vance and the other man's holding him erect. For a moment he weakly tried breaking away, but then abruptly he gave in and let them lead him across to the buggy and help him up into it. He sank back against the seat, muttering: "You and me, Vance, we could. . . ."

Whatever his thought he didn't complete it, but there was enough meaning to his words to make Rita Kirby eye Vance with a wondering, puzzled look. He was very aware of her closeness, of her lithe slenderness, and of the beauty of her face set in such seriousness as she asked in a hushed, frightened way: "What's wrong with him? His face . . . and the way he talks. . . ."

"He's going to be all right," Vance said, shaking his head to warn her that she was saying the wrong thing.

Childers said quickly: "You should've seen I it, Rita. There was this gun pointed straight at him and then. . . ."

Once again his words trailed off so that the meaning behind them was obscure and Rita, now halfway understanding the urgency of Fred's glance, said quickly: "Joe, take Bill's horse on in."

"Better let me stay with you."

"No. You go on. Get some water heating in the kitchen. And hurry!"

Her tone sent Joe across to Bill's horse at once, and, as he went to the saddle and started away, Rita nodded to Vance and stepped on out to the edge of the road behind the buggy.

When he had followed and was standing beside her, she said: "Now tell me."

"Let Bill tell it. You're wasting time."

She looked up at him, eyes bright with anger. "You did this to him?"

"No."

"Then who did?"

"A hardcase by the name of Spane."

"Jeff Spane?" she breathed almost inaudibly. "How . . . ?"

"All this talk won't do Bill any good," Vance reminded her.

Now the anger seemed to leave her and he heard her sigh in a baffled way as she started back to the buggy. He followed, giving her a hand as she climbed the step to the seat alongside Childers. Before she could sit back, he had to reach and push Childers out of the way.

She unwound the reins from the whip socket, her hands shaking. Then, about to speak to the team, she hesitated and looked down at him. "I don't know why you've done this," she said in a low voice. "But I'm grateful. Very."

A smile broke across his lean face. "It's a good thing your father isn't listening," he drawled. "By the way, has Sayers got the whole town out after me?"

"Dad didn't say. He was with the sheriff when I left."

"You can tell him I've moved in at Stirrup."

She stared across at him speculatively. "Do you expect to stay?"

He laughed, shaking his head. "That depends on a few things, Miss Kirby."

She tightened the reins now, still looking at him, saying deliberately: "At any rate I wish you luck, Fred Vance."

"Much obliged. I may need it."

She slapped the team into motion now, and, as the buggy pulled away, she looked around at him, hardly yet believing that this was happening to her, that Vance had had the cool nerve to ride this close to Box.

She watched his tall shape, standing there in the road, until the night swallowed him, and then turned and looked at Bill. His weight was sagging heavily against her shoulder. For the first time now she saw his face closely and the shock of seeing its disfigurement brought on a real panic in her. A dark stain showed against the light cloth of her coat. She knew it was blood. She reached for the whip then.

Now and then, as the buggy rattled along the road, she could hear Bill's labored breathing and that heightened her fear until she wondered if he would be alive when the drive was over. When she finally turned in along the lane of poplars below the house, she had the team at a run.

They were waiting for her at the yard gate, Foster and Zinn and Red, the ones who should have been at Stirrup, and Joe Banks. As she stood aside, letting them lift Bill out of the buggy, she held back the questions she wanted to ask. She told them— "Take him to his room."—before she ran up to the kitchen.

A kettle was boiling on the stove. She found some clean rags in one of the cupboards. Crossing the yard to the porch fronting Bill's room in the short wing of the house, she saw that his doorway was lighted now and that the others stood, waiting at the foot of the steps.

It was Foster who said as she passed him: "He won't let us touch him, miss. You may need help."

"I'll manage," she answered.

Joe Banks moved out of the doorway to let her into the room. Bill was standing by the marble-topped washstand. His shirt was off and he was bent over, sloshing water from the basin onto his face. He heard her come in and turned away to reach for a towel and covered his face with it before he turned to say gruffly: "I'll do this myself, Rita."

She carried the kettle and rags over and put them on the washstand. Then she looked at him in a pleading way. "Please, Bill, let me help."

He shook his head.

She sensed that she could accomplish nothing by insisting, so as she slowly backed toward the door, she asked: "Are you going to tell me about Fred Vance?"

Interest came alive in his eyes and he forgot to keep his battered face covered as he said: "You should've seen him. There's a man to take along. Waded right in and. . . ."

His words broke off abruptly as a heavy tread crossed the porch. She could no longer look at his face, so glanced toward the door, surprised to see that it was her father.

Kirby stopped barely across the threshold, rage patterning his craggy face. But what he saw shocked him and his look softened. "Good God, man! They didn't tell me it was this bad!"

Bill remembered the towel now and covered his face again, and, when he didn't speak, Kirby gave Rita an amazed look, asking: "Was it Vance?"

"No." It was Bill who answered him. "Vance helped me, got me out of a damned tight spot."

"Then who was it?"

Bill shook his head tiredly. "Jim, I'm played out. Let me alone, will you?"

Kirby said stubbornly: "We're going back there after Vance."

Bill again moved his head from side to side. "Not me."

"Of course not you. There's six of us without you."

"It won't do you any good. Vance won't be there now."

Kirby swore acidly and, turning to go out again, snapped: "Rita, look after him."

Bill stood, eyeing the door for several seconds after it had closed behind Kirby. At length his glance moved around to Rita. "He's not going to like this," he said deliberately. "But I'm pulling out."

Her expression had been tender and full of sympathy. But now his words jarred her, turned her wide-eyed. "Leaving?"

He nodded. "Tonight. Now."

"Bill, you can't!"

Her helpless, stunned look made him say quickly, savagely almost: "Just let it go at that, Rita. I'm quitting. Maybe I'll be back. You can tell Jim that."

"But . . . ," she began helplessly. "You're hurt, Bill. Badly."

"I've got my second wind now."

"Dad can't get along without you."

"Foster knows the ropes well enough."

A subtle change turned her glance into one that seemed to probe at his innermost thoughts as she said gently: "There's something you're not telling us, Bill."

"About Spane? Ask the others."

"I don't mean that. There's something else. Something about Fred Vance."

She knows, he was telling himself as he finally found it impossible to meet her glance any longer and turned away.

"Can you tell me about it?" she asked quietly.

"Look, Rita." He wondered if he could tell her of the difference this night had made in his way of looking at things. Just a minute ago the coolness of the water against his face had chilled the fever from his brain and he had been able to see the last hour and a half in its proper perspective. He wanted very much to tell her his thoughts now, wanted her to understand them, for her opinion meant a great deal. But then he knew that until he understood those thoughts himself, there was no possible way of explaining them. So he said wearily: "Did you ever have a knot tied up inside you and not be able to jerk it loose?"

"Perhaps. I know what you mean."

"You have to get it untied, don't you? Well, that's why I'm leaving."

He had hoped without quite knowing how it would come about that he could get away without seeing Jim Kirby again.

But now that hope died as Kirby's solid steps crossed the porch once more and the man's huge shape moved in through the door.

Kirby was furious, that much was at once obvious even before he asked sharply: "What's this about Spane? What's that mangy little four-flusher trying to do to us?"

"He thought he was working for Vance," Bill told him. "He isn't any more."

Kirby's exasperation made him say: "You're talking hogwash."

"That's all I know, Jim. Spane came in there to move us out, claiming Vance had hired him. Then Vance showed up and sided with me against him, kicked him off the place."

"None of that makes sense."

"So it doesn't." Bill shrugged. "But that's what happened."

He'd suddenly had enough of Kirby's dictatorial manner and now he pulled on his shirt and stepped around the big man and to the door.

"Where are you going?" Kirby wanted to know.

"Out. Ask Rita about it." And Bill hurried on across the porch and down the steps.

Kirby started to follow, and Rita said quickly: "Let him alone, Dad." Passing him on her way to the door, she touched his arm and gave him a fleeting smile to take the sting from her words. Then she hurried on out after Bill, who was crossing the yard toward the barn.

He heard her coming and stopped, facing around to say quietly: "I was counting on you. Now you're making it harder."

"I'm not trying to stop you, Bill. But there's something you should know before you leave . . . if you're going to see Fred Vance."

"What?" He straightened a little in his surprise, and although the shadows didn't let her see much, she judged that his swollen face had relaxed out of its angry set.

"I'll leave it to you what to tell him. But I was there in Ben Sayers's office with Dad when they made their plans. Ben has taken four men up to watch Summit and the pass trails. Harry Wilson and two others are to the south along the Bearpaw. Dad is supposed to be keeping an eye on Stirrup."

He was looking at her fixedly and it was a long moment before he spoke. "Why would you be wanting to do this for Vance?"

"You'll be doing it, Bill, not me," she answered hesitantly.

Although she wouldn't have believed it possible, his misshapen face actually took on a smile now. "Rita," he said, "you should've been a man." And with these enigmatic words he turned and left her.

He was thankful no one was at the corral to hound him with questions. He hurried, fearing someone would come down there and try to stop him. He caught up the first animal that would stand and take the bridle. Only when he had saddled and was riding out the lane did the tension drain away and let him really feel the throbbing of his head again.

The ride back to Stirrup seemed longer than the one he had made this way with Vance, yet he was feeling stronger and, for a private reason, keyed up by having found the nerve to quit Kirby. Yesterday, even two hours ago, the possibility of leaving Box would have seemed ridiculous. Yet here he was, on his own by choice.

He was within sight of the dark shadow of the cottonwoods lying against the paler pattern of Stirrup's lower meadow when he had the awesome thought: *Maybe I'll have to clear out after all.* That sobered him so that as he rode in on the darkened layout he was thinking straighter than he had been.

First he went to the corral. It was open, empty, and that was disappointing. Remembering what an effort it was to walk, he stayed in the saddle and rode back up to the crew quarters.

He reined in within a few strides of the door and sat, listening a moment. No sound came to him. He caught the taint of coal oil in the air and would have smiled but for the aching of his face.

He drew in a deep breath finally and called: "Vance!"

The echo of his voice, shuttling back from the barn, held a hollow, feeble note. He was all at once feeling very much alone.

"Vance!" he called again.

Abruptly he heard a sound behind him. It came from the direction of the wagon shed. He turned in the saddle and saw Fred Vance's tall shape coming toward him out of the shadows. He pulled the horse on around so that he faced Vance. And now that dread loneliness had left him.

He wondered how he could say what he wanted to say and his search for words was futile. In the end he stated simply: "I'm back."

Vance had stopped and was looking up. He shook his head slowly. "Don't make me do it, Bill. You're inside my fence and you don't belong. No one from Box does. I thought you knew that."

"I do," Bill said quietly. "I've quit Kirby."

"You've what?" Vance's tone was awed.

"Quit. I'm here to stay, Vance. If you'll have me." The starlight let Bill see the reserve that settled across Vance's face and he said urgently: "It's no trick! No one sent me. I'm here to side you. I want a job, any job."

"Why?" came Vance's toneless query.

"You saved my hide tonight."

"That's not reason enough."

"Then I'm sick of swinging the whip for Kirby. Put it that way."

"That's better." Vance was silent a moment, peering up intently at the man. "They'll be on my tail, Bill. It'll be long hours and cold camps. Maybe they'll run me out."

"Like hell they will!"

Now a slow, broad smile softened the angles of Vance's face. And he said gently: "Better light and come inside. We'll see if there's any coffee."

Bill Childers was grateful for the way Vance stepped on past him then and into the bunkhouse, leaving him alone. He was also thankful for the darkness. He wasn't a man who often let another see this much of his feelings and he badly needed this solitary interval that was letting him get a grip on himself.

CHAPTER NINE

Rita Kirby was wakened with the dawn next morning by her father's heavy step along the hallway. She lay, dozing for several minutes, vaguely hearing the clatter of dishes and pans sounding from the kitchen, wondering why the cook was up and around at this ungodly hour. Then she remembered. The crew would be going across to Stirrup.

She got up at once, and by the time she came into the dining room Jim Kirby was just leaving the table, his breakfast finished and his early morning cigar already lit.

She said: "Give me two minutes and I'll ride as far as the forks with you, Dad." On her way across to the kitchen door, she noticed his scowl and stopped. "Are you in too much of a hurry?"

"No." His glance dropped to her waist. She was wearing a plaid calico shirt, boots, and a pair of clean but worn waist overalls Joe Banks, the wrangler, had swapped her for a pair of spur leathers. Now she knew what was bothering her father even before he said sternly: "It's unbecoming of a lady to be gotten up like a man, Rita. Better change to a skirt."

"But I'm going across to see Lola and Tom. That's too far to ride with your leg wound around a side-saddle. If you don't believe me, try it." And with a smile she went on into the kitchen.

By the time she ran down to the corral, Foster had her paint saddled and ready. There were four more of the crew ready to ride, Joe Banks, Red Durns, Mel West, and old Charley Simpson. As they started out the lane, she came in beside her father to ask mischievously: "Do you think you're taking enough men, Dad?"

He eyed her obliquely in a severe way. "Bill needs more help over there."

"So he does."

His glance sharpened. "Just what do you mean by that?"

"Nothing." She was regretting her levity now. "You said Bill needed more help. I agreed."

"Do you think I'm letting Vance scare me off?" he bridled.

"No. You'll stay on Stirrup even if you run short of help here."

"Is anything wrong with that?"

"Dad," she said mildly, "you're right in every way. And it's too nice a day to spoil by arguing."

He rode on in sullen silence, hanging back out of the others' dust. But he was worrying the thing about in his mind. He was much in need of Rita's opinion on a certain matter and, knowing she had a mind of her own much like her mother had had before her, he finally chose a different and a milder approach.

"I'd certainly like to know what was stuck in his craw last night," was how he put it.

She simply nodded. She didn't ask who he was talking about, in fact didn't say anything. That made him burst out: "Good Lord, I pay him as much as any ranch boss in the territory and he leaves me flat when I need him most!"

Rita gave him an oddly speculative glance. "Money doesn't buy everything, Jim."

Her "Jim" gave him warning; only when she was utterly grave or when she was in a nice way trying to tell him he'd done something wrong did she ever call him that. It sobered him now, made him ask: "Just what have I done to him, girl? Just what?"

"It isn't what you've done, Dad. It's what Fred Vance has done."

"And what has he done?"

She only shook her head and stood in the stirrups to push her horse on faster, and, as she drew on ahead, he sensed that she was trying to avoid saying anything that would hurt his feelings. That roused his stubbornness and he reined on beside her again, asking doggedly: "What has Vance done?"

She gave him a helpless look. "I don't know what's wrong with Bill, Dad. I honestly don't. If you made me say what I'm thinking, it would only make you angry. Anyway, I'm just guessing."

"Then guess out loud. I'm trying to get to the bottom of this."

Once more they slowed their animals, letting Foster and the others draw away. And presently Rita looked around at him. "I think Bill's ashamed of what you're doing to Vance. Just that, nothing more. I think he respects Vance more than he does . . . more than. . . ."

"More than he does me?" Kirby growled.

"No. Not that. Bill respects you. What I was going to say is that perhaps Bill respects Vance more than he does himself. There's a way of looking at this that makes it seem you're not being quite fair with Fred Vance, that Bill himself isn't."

"Is a man to be respected when he hires a known rustler, maybe a killer, to work for him?"

"No, Dad. I'm not thinking of that."

"Do you know Jeff Spane? Have you ever laid eyes on him?"

"I have. He sat opposite me in the stage coming across from Dry Wells that time last summer. He's a poor specimen."

A moment ago Kirby had been holding a tight rein on his unstable temper. But now quite suddenly his anger left him. "So I'm not being fair with Vance. You're thinking of my taking out that warrant on him?"

"That to begin with."

"You must not think he killed Milt."

"I don't. You don't, either. Nor does Bill."

He couldn't keep a straight face. "All right, that point's yours. Let's say I have my doubts. If I didn't, the whole crew would have gone back there last night instead of waiting till now. Keeping Vance locked up in jail was just a way of cooling him off so he could see the sense of this lease."

"It didn't cool him much. He's no longer locked up. He outbluffed our men once, and he can do it again. So where are you?"

"To tell the truth, Rita, exactly where I started."

"You're not even that far. To begin with you had a chance for the lease. Now you've lost it. You've made an enemy of Fred Vance. He can make you so miserable you'll be wishing you'd never thought of the lease."

He eyed her with an open respect. "That's something I'd like your opinion on. If you were Vance, how would you go about making me eat crow?"

"Why, I'd . . . I'd probably cut fence and start pushing your cattle off the place."

"I've thought of that. I'll put fence riders out. What else?"

She lifted her square shoulders. "Vance doesn't have anything to lose. You've made it so. He can come in at night and shoot the windows out of the bunkhouse. He could . . . there are any number of things he could do, Dad. You lose regardless of what he does."

"I've thought of that, too." He was quite serious now. "So how would you go about it if you were me?"

"The way Bill's doing. Make my peace with him. Let him have Stirrup."

His jaw tightened and that anger she knew so well flashed in his eyes. "That I won't do!"

"In that case I have no suggestions to offer, Senator."

"Don't make a joke of it," he said severely, his frown reprimanding her. "I can beat him in the courts."

"Can you? And still do what you'd like to do in Washington? You'll have to be here to testify, you know. The hearing may come at an awkward time."

"Keely's going to rush this case through now. We can still stay over another week and give me time for everything that needs doing back East."

She smiled at him in a pitying way. "This will take longer than a week, Dad."

He fell silent again, staring vacantly ahead, and when Rita saw that they were coming up on the side trail that swung east into the higher hills, she halfway thought of going on with him to Stirrup and riding to Cross D the long way. But the day was too pleasant to be spoiled by prolonging this worry over her father's affairs; besides, she was eager to see Tom.

So as they came up on the forks, she told him: "Don't look for me before the middle of the afternoon."

He stopped, eyeing her speculatively. "So you don't think Bill will be there?"

"Did I say I thought that?"

"No, but you do." He waited. When she said nothing, he asked: "Want to make a bet on it?"

"I hope he is there, Dad. For your sake."

"But you don't think he will be. Come on, here's your chance to make an honest dollar." He smiled meagerly. "I say Bill hasn't quit me. You think he has. Are you sure enough of your hunch to put up your two best steers against any two of mine you want to pick?"

Years ago on the Christmas, when Rita had been eight, her father had given her a dozen heifers as a present. They had been branded with a Box M, the M for Marguerite. Since then his crew had put that brand on each of her calves. Her herd had multiplied; she had added to it out of the proceeds of selling off the old and poor animals. Last fall her tally had run nearly a seventh of the total on Box. Now she was paying the wages of one crewman out of her own pocket. So she was in a position to cover his wager.

She thought about it a moment, eyeing him amusedly. "Why be a piker, Dad? You're so sure, let's make it five."

"Five it is." He held out his hand. Things were always man-fashion between them.

That handshake went beyond the sealing of their bargain. Rita knew that it was intended to smooth over their disagreement. Her father was always that way, sorry afterward for his outbursts of temper, eager to make amends. And now, as they parted, she watched him run his horse on after the others. When he turned finally and waved, she took it as meaning that he was over his grouch.

By the time she rode into the timber, climbing now, her mood was lighter and she was beginning to enjoy the day. The cool piney sweetness of the air, the bright dappled sunlight slanting through the trees, brought a slow exhilaration that washed her mind clean of the troubles of last night and this morning. Yet she had a hard time dismissing her curiosity about Bill Childers. It was strangely heartening to suppose that he was with Fred Vance; it gave her a guilty feeling to realize that in wishing Bill well she was being a little disloyal to her father. But from the moment she had learned that Vance wouldn't lease, she had been against trying to hold Stirrup.

She was wishing now that Bill had told her more about last night, or that she had insisted on Vance telling her what had happened. At first it had seemed incongruous to think of Fred Vance helping Bill Childers or any other Box man. But now she had the disquieting conviction that this was exactly the thing one might expect of him. She didn't know why she thought this of him, for her upbringing had taught her an outright dislike of his very name. Still, she did realize that it had taken some downright nerve for him to bring Bill across from Stirrup last night when he must have known that not only the sheriff but Jim Kirby would be hunting him.

But at the moment she wanted to forget the Stirrup trouble, to forget Bill Childers and Vance, Spane, her father's indecision. And she finally did close her mind to all these things. When, after riding steadily for half an hour, she came to the clearing in which sat the ruin of Dean's abandoned homestead cabin above The Springs, she stopped and got down to pick some of the wild flowers that streaked the clearing with myriad color.

It was while she kneeled there, making up a bouquet for Lola, that she heard ever so faintly a sound that might have been the distant crackle of rifle fire. But then a light breeze ran up the slope, laying a whisper through the tops of the pines. After she had paused to listen for several more seconds, hearing nothing but the wind, her momentary uneasiness left her.

CHAPTER TEN

It was Vance, standing in the doorway of the kitchen lean-to while he drank the last of his breakfast coffee, who saw the dust far out along the south slope and drawled: "Visitors, Bill."

Childers got up from the table and came to stand behind him, looking out over his shoulder and trying to open his bad eye wider. Except for two ugly red gashes and the swelling on that side of his face, plus his nose being a good deal wider than usual, the beating had done him no harm beyond what a couple more nights of solid sleep wouldn't cure.

"That'll be Kirby," Bill said shortly.

Vance nodded. He turned into the room, put his cup on the table, and eyed Bill soberly. "Now's your last chance to change your mind, friend."

Bill grunted his disgust. "Save your talk for when it'll count. What do we do, get out or hang on?"

Vance stood, staring out through the doorway at that plume of dust in the south. Some thought finally gave his blue eyes an amused glint and he said: "We get out. But we have some fun on the way."

"How?"

Vance explained, and presently they left the kitchen and went to the corral for their horses. It was Bill who finally led the two saddled animals up into the cottonwoods behind the house and tied them. By the time he was back again, Vance was roping two blanket rolls and shortly carried them to the window alongside the double bunks to drop them outside. Bill had meantime lifted down a Winchester over the head of his bed and pulled another from a disorderly pile of gear in the far corner, drawling: "Red won't be needing this."

They found a box of shells on the sill of the front window, and, as they stood there, looking out, Vance rolled up a smoke and passed his tobacco across. Childers divided his glance about evenly between his hands and the bottom of the meadow, where Kirby and his five crewmen were now following the trail as it angled out from the pines.

Presently Bill said acidly: "He's so damned sure of himself."

Vance didn't speak for several seconds. Then he asked: "Which one will be the hardest to scare?"

"Kirby."

"Who after him?"

"Foster. The one on the claybank."

"You can take Kirby then, I take Foster. When they get to this side of the rock."

The "rock" was a granite shelf, an outcropping some three feet high, around which the trail bent before lining straight for the corrals. It was nearly two hundred yards away, and now, as Red and Foster in the lead turned past it, Bill hefted the .30-30 up and laid it across the window sill.

Vance moved less hastily, saying: "Let 'em come on a bit. And remember, low."

Shortly he had Foster in the notch of the carbine's sight. He let the front sight drop then, eased out half a breath, and said: "Now."

A split second before the weapon jarred his shoulder, Bill's exploded sharply. He saw the puff of dust spring up two feet out from the left front hoof of Foster's horse as he was levering in another shell. He laid his sights again, eased on the trigger as a rider wheeled into line, then squeezed off the next shot. It was a moment before he caught the shrill whine of his bullet ricocheting from the face of the outcropping. Alongside him Bill Childers started laughing.

Vance stood watching and enjoying it as Bill threw three more shots. Foster had slammed into the man behind him and his horse was bucking off the trail and away from the others who were running for the rock and away from Kirby, who was standing fast. The first man to reach the outcropping vaulted from the saddle and let his animal go on, diving for cover. Kirby was backing that way, having a hard time managing his nervous animal as he pulled a Winchester from the scabbard under his leg. A voice shouting in anger carried in over the distance and Vance guessed it was Kirby as the man turned finally and ran on past the outcropping, leading Foster and one other away.

Those three stopped well down the meadow, a good four hundred yards below, and, as the two Box men rode up to Kirby, Vance could see him pointing off toward the trees. Then shortly Foster and the other man headed across there with their horses at a run.

"Time to go," Vance said.

A sudden burst of blue smoke showed to one side of the outcropping now and before the sound of the shot reached them there came the solid thunk of the bullet striking the door frame. That hurried Bill as he followed Vance across the room and out the back window. As they picked up their blanket rolls and started running for their horses tied beyond the cotton-woods, another shot hit the nearly empty pail by the door and it fell, banging, to the ground.

They stayed out of sight by keeping in line with the building until the trees hid them, a rattle of gunfire rising out of the meadow below now. Vance was settling into the saddle when he heard one of the front windows go out with a jangling of glass. Alongside him, Bill said: "They'll play hell with your bunkhouse before they catch onto it."

After they had ridden a hundred yards up toward the meadow, Vance swung over into the timber. Presently he pulled the sorrel down to a walk and sat half turned, listening. The sound he was expecting didn't come for a full quarter minute and then it came suddenly. There was a breaking of branches far below, then a reckless hoof drum rose over the racket of gunfire. A voice called something unintelligible there and some moments later a rifle cracked much closer than the others. Soon a second joined it.

Bill looked at Vance, grinning and shaking his head. The matting of pine needles on the ground muffled the sound of their animals' walking as they started away. The shots, near and far, continued sporadically.

From the trees at the head of the meadow they finally glimpsed Foster and the other Box man shooting from behind a windfall at the rear windows of the bunkhouse. Jim Kirby had finally managed to surround the empty layout.

When Vance had seen enough, he said: "Now we'll look for Josh Hawks."

They started up through the pines, Bill Childers's swollen face set in a satisfied smile. It had been a long time since he'd enjoyed anything this much.

CHAPTER ELEVEN

Two miles above Dean's homestead ruin the trail to Cross D traveled a shallow draw for some distance, presently cutting up a steep and sandy bank to a hummock studded with a thin growth of cedar. Rita gave her horse his head and he slogged into the upgrade at a slow, soundless walk. As she topped the rise, she was looking off through the trees toward an open grassy stretch paralleling the trail ahead.

She didn't see the two men at first, for their animals were standing against the dark backdrop of the timber on the far side of the open ground. But then abruptly one horse moved so that the white blaze on his chest showed plainly. The animal was as surely Tom Demmler's bay as was the stocky shape in the saddle Tom's.

Rita scarcely looked at the second man in her delight at this prospect of making the rest of the ride with Tom. She had ridden on part way through the trees, going toward the two, when the second man came lazily aground and stood, looking up at Tom, evidently talking to him. And in that instant she recognized Jeff Spane and brought her horse quickly to a stand.

She reined back behind a tree, then wheeled and turned down into the draw again, for a moment too surprised to think of anything but of getting out of sight, telling herself that she couldn't embarrass Tom by riding up to him when he was in the company of such a notoriously questionable character as Spane. He had every right to be there with Spane, of course.

Some simple, straightforward explanation lay behind their being together. They had probably been traveling the trail in opposite directions, had met and stopped to have a smoke, and yarn a while. Rita had lived long enough in this country to know that such meetings were often unavoidable.

Back in the draw again, she climbed along it for several hundred yards, until she knew she was well above Tom and Spane. Then she cut obliquely across into the timber and, after holding this direction for possibly five minutes, swung down until she cut the trail again.

She went on slowly, hoping Tom would overtake her. But then within another mile she came to Cross D's fence, went through the gate, and shortly had the layout in sight. She rode on in with a real regret, the prospect of visiting with Lola a decided let-down.

When she came to the porch, she called Lola's name and got no answer. She stepped from the saddle onto the porch and went to the open door, and called again. Still there was no answer.

Knowing Lola must be away, she went on in, pausing a moment in the living room to enjoy its freshness and bright color. Going to the kitchen, she put the flowers in a jar and brought them back to the big table in the main room. It was then that the idea of surprising Tom came to her.

She led the horse out back and up into the trees behind the root cellar, tying him, feeling a keen disappointment over the possibility that Tom might perhaps be gone for the day. Back in the house again she was feeling restless, undecided as to what to do. The kitchen was clean, everything in order, not even so much as a plate on the table to let her guess what Tom's or Lola's plans for the day might be. She sauntered out onto the porch and sat at its edge, an idle glance at the sun telling her that the morning was better than half gone. A jay, hopping upward along the branches of a spruce close by, began scolding her. She was feeling out of sorts, her disappointment keen.

Perhaps that mood was the reason for her seeing what she did as she looked down at the corral and the barn. She had been here only twice before and both times in Tom's company, enjoying every minute of her stay. She had found the cabin pleasant, Lola's cooking a rare treat. If she had ever noticed anything but the house except in a superficial way she couldn't recall it.

But now her critical eye picked out several things about the place that were disconcerting. The hay rake, for instance, sat rusting in the open, while thirty feet away the open-sided barn's runway stood empty of everything but a pile of harness lying near the door. The harness shouldn't be there, of course. Neither should the empty cans and the broken bottles be littering the space between the barn's end and a nearby shed. The tin roof of that shed was loose at one corner—probably the wind had worked the nails out—and curled up so that whatever was stored inside was exposed to the elements. It would have taken a man only a few minutes' work to fix it.

She caught herself just then, thinking irritably: *You're anything but perfect, so why take it out on Tom!* And to forestall any further faultfinding she went inside again. There was a shelf of books and periodicals over the settee. She found a pattern book and sat down with it, and, when the sound of a horse on the way up the trail reached her nearly an hour later, she was deeply engrossed in Godey's design for a velveteen afternoon dress.

It was Tom. Rita stood back out of sight at the door as she remembered how she'd hidden the horse. Her surprise would be complete. And all at once she was happy again and smiling.

She watched him turn the bay into the corral and carry his saddle out, closing the gate. Then, when he abruptly dropped the saddle, letting it fall into the dust, her smile went away. She had always been taught to look after things and what he did now only reminded her of the things she had noticed earlier.

But then she saw the head down and brooding way he was sauntering up the path toward the house, and in wondering at it she forgot the other. That he had something on his mind was quite obvious. His manner sobered her, took away her light-heartedness. Now suddenly she decided it would be unfair to surprise him so completely.

So she called out when he was coming up on the rose arbor at the foot of the path. He came to a quick halt and his head lifted in amazement. Then a slow smile broke across his face.

"Rita!" He was delighted and hurried up the path to the foot of the steps. "Would you believe it? I was on my way up here to grab a bite and then get across to see you. Talk about luck, mine's in!"

"You've even got a cook," she said.

"Where's Lola?"

"Not here."

"Then we'll eat up everything good we can find."

"Let's!" He came up beside her, full of eagerness now, took her hand, and led her on through the living room and into the kitchen. "Lola's got some strawberries hid somewhere. And I cut steaks last night. There are eggs and. . . ."

"And that's enough, Tom!"

He laughed and started for the door leading out onto the stoop. It was then that she suddenly remembered he hadn't heard about last night, and before she had quite thought it out, she was saying: "Tom, did you know that Fred Vance broke out of jail yesterday?"

He stopped in the doorway, turning slowly. "Fred what?"

"Broke jail. Dad was with him in the sheriff's office and. . . ."

A thought cut her short. *But he's seen Spane and Spane knows!*

"Then what?" Tom asked, coming back into the room.

In her confusion Rita made the best of it, saying after only a slight hesitation: "He got out the window and away before they could stop him. And that's not all," she added, trying to believe that he was really as surprised as he looked.

"Not all? You mean there's more?"

His question was so absolutely guileless that she told herself he couldn't possibly know about this. Spane naturally wouldn't have mentioned it. So now her keen relief brought her words in a rush: "Last night he was at Stirrup with that Jeff Spane. Spane was evidently working for him. Bill Childers was badly beaten and. . . ."

"No!"

That one explosive word and his contrite look made her ask quickly: "What have I said, Tom?"

"It isn't what you've said," he told her ruefully. "It's what I've done. This . . . it's probably all my fault, Rita. You say Bill took a bad beating?"

"Yes." She studied him questioningly until she realized he might notice something strange in her. "But why say it's your fault?"

"Fred wanted a crew, asked me to find some men. Men who would play it rough, he said. I couldn't think of anyone who'd fit that order better than Spane. So night before last I rode up to Summit and hired him to bring a crew down. Now he's gone hog wild, has he?" She was staring at him so oddly that after a moment he asked: "What's wrong, Rita?"

"You didn't . . . didn't know what Spane had done last night?"

He lifted his hands outward in an unknowing gesture. The answer she was praying he wouldn't give came then. "How could I know?"

Rita stood speechless, her doubt suddenly real and engulfing all her thoughts. She felt weak and overwhelmed by Tom's denial. As she stared at him, wide-eyed, her face losing color, he seemed all at once a different man.

Only when he said with abrupt concern—"Rita, you're pale."—and stepped toward her did she realize she must hide her emotion.

She gave an uneasy laugh and reached up and ran a hand across her forehead. "Too much of the sun, probably. I should have worn a hat."

"Here." He pulled a chair over and made her sit in it. He brought her a cup of water, and she drank every drop of it although she wasn't thirsty, drank it slowly so that she would have time to think. It gave her an excuse for not speaking; it was something to distract him while she regained her self-control.

When she finally set the cup aside, her thoughts were steadier and she realized she must somehow hide her doubt until she understood it. The best way of doing that, she decided, was to avoid the subject that had brought it on. Only in that way would Tom believe her explanation of what had caused the sudden change in her.

So now she said: "That's better. But about Fred Vance, Tom. They're hunting him. Dad was furious. He's even thinking of offering a reward."

"He's making a mistake if he does." His look was still full of concern and he asked: "You're sure you're all right?"

She nodded. "You know how much Dad listens to anyone. Another thing that's upset him is losing Bill Childers." At his surprised look she went on to tell him of last night. But she didn't mention that she suspected Bill was with Vance, an uneasy instinct cautioning her against confiding too much in him.

What she had to say seemed to please him, and, when she had finished, he told her quite soberly: "If Childers has quit, you won't keep the others for long. Fred's dead serious about this, Rita. He'll fight if you drive him to it."

"Dad's finding that out."

"Then why doesn't your father pull in his horns, tear up that warrant, and move out of Stirrup?"

She smiled and shook her head, coming out of her chair now and going to the shelf in the corner of the room to take down plates and silverware. As she set them on the table, she said: "When you find out how my father's mind works, I wish you'd explain it to me, Tom. But can't we forget all this before it spoils our day?" She glanced toward the back door. "You're forgetting the strawberries. And we need cream."

The several minutes he was gone let her get a better hold on herself and, having led him away from the subject, when he came back in, she at once mentioned something else. By the time they sat down to the meal, Tom seemed in good spirits again and she had decided she was being extremely foolish.

Some simple explanation lay behind what now appeared to be his out-and-out lie; she wouldn't believe he had deliberately deceived her. So she put all thought of what he had said aside, postponing any attempt at reasoning it out.

The awkwardness between them was gone and only once over the two hours they were together did he again mention the Stirrup trouble. They were sitting at the edge of the porch, watching the clouds building up over the peaks close to the east and he was telling her of his plans for the lease. He had been saying he would stock his eastern end of Stirrup by buying culls from a Texas herd due to arrive within the next two weeks at a reservation agency thirty miles south of Lodgepole. Then, abruptly, his look of eagerness faded before a worried one that prompted her to say: "Yes, Tom. And then?"

He shook his head. "What's the use of planning? Before any of this can happen, I'll have to find Fred and help him get squared away. Which puts me on the other side of the fence from Jim Kirby."

"Lots of people are on the opposite side of the fence from Dad, Tom."

He gave her a grateful look, one that thanked her for her understanding, and in that moment he seemed so likable and straightforward that she wondered what inane twisting of words had ever made her doubt him. She was on the point of asking him outright how it happened he hadn't known about Fred Vance when he had seen Spane this morning, but the impulse died before her desire that nothing should spoil this pleasant interval.

Finally Rita took warning from the eastward-tipping shadows and told him she must go. "Then I'll come along a couple miles with you," he said. "If Fred's on the loose, one sure way of finding him is to find Hawks. So I'll take a look up Squaw."

CHAPTER TWELVE

Standing at Stirrup's main corral and looking up northeastward to the peaks, a man with a knowing eye could pick out a short white scar lined across the bright green of the aspen forest that was the final bend of the Summit road close below timberline and the settlement. If he knew where to look, he could also see, straight to the east, a pale blue patch lying low against the black shoulder of the highest alp, Sentinel Peak. This was a fringe of spruce edging the rim directly above Demmler's Cross D. The country in between was isolated, wild, crossed two-thirds of the way by but one trail that ended at Anderson's homestead.

Midway between these two points a craggy knob jutted out from the mountain. For three hours now, Fred Vance had been sitting with his back to a ledge along the face of the promontory. The sorrel was tied immediately below and out of sight in the pines. Bill Childers was down somewhere along Squaw looking for Josh Hawks, his tiredness and soreness making him glad to have been spared the hard climb with Vance.

Several times over this long interval Vance had longed for a pair of field glasses. Every detail of the low country was spread out before him. He had seen the comings and goings of several riders and knew generally that he must be responsible for some of them being on the move—the ones cruising up and down the Summit road particularly. Yet the distance was too great for him to recognize a single man.

He had particularly watched the two horsemen who had come

closest to him during the middle afternoon, following the trail that ended at Anderson's. The homestead down there was new since his day, and he idly wondered just who the man could be who had cleared land and built a cabin in this high country where until now the Demmlers had had things to themselves. Anderson's clearing lay a little better than a mile below and to the north and was plainly in sight. He had seen the two riders stop there to be met by a man who walked up from the barn. The three stood by their horses, evidently talking for some minutes, and were presently joined by two women who came out of the cabin.

Some twenty minutes after they had ridden into the clearing the pair went on, cutting off through the forest in the direction of the Summit road. Now and then Vance sighted them as they topped a rise or crossed an open stretch and finally, certain they weren't swinging back in his direction, he lost interest in them. It was shortly after this that he saw one of the women ride away from the cabin and out the trail in his direction.

He watched her coming on now, incuriously sighting her several times through the downward pines. After several minutes she rode into the open again, starting across the foot of the slope directly below where a collapsed rim had uprooted all but a few big ponderosas. It was when she came out into the strong sunlight that he gave a start and sat straighter. Even at this distance her bright sorrel hair was unmistakable. She must be Lola Demmler.

A thought struck him that at once brought him to his feet and sent him hurrying to his horse. He ran the animal recklessly down through the pines, and, when he came to the trail, she was in sight, climbing a long aisle through the aspen trees toward him.

She must have caught the racket he made coming down through the timber for, shortly after he appeared, she drew rein and sat there, looking at him, and the thought struck him: *She doesn't know me from Adam.*

He started toward her and immediately she reined her horse halfway around, still looking back at him, leaning forward in the side-saddle as though ready to put her horse into a run back along the trail. He called—"Lola?"—and at once saw her settle back out of her rigid attitude.

He recognized her now, and, when he was close enough to read her expression, he could see that it was a blend of puzzlement and alarm. So he again spoke. "You don't know me, do . . . ?"

"Fred!"

Her startled exclamation cut him short. Then, as he came in and stopped close in front of her, she gave him a look of outright gladness that at once took on concern. She turned and looked back down the trail in a wary way, saying quickly: "Get out of sight! Ben Sayers and another man have just ridden through here."

"I know. They kept straight on." He tilted his head toward the high granite shoulder above. "I watched from up there."

Her apprehension left her then and she was smiling, her violet eyes showing an open interest in him. "Now that I know what you look like, I can understand."

"Understand what, Lola?"

"How Kirby was tricked this morning." Suddenly she was laughing. "Did you know he sent a man for the sheriff, that he waited until Sayers had arrived before they stopped shooting up the place, and went in to find no one there?"

"No." He chuckled with a genuine amusement. "That was too good a play to let pass. But we didn't think it was that good."

"Is Bill Childers with you?"

She was serious again, surprisingly so, and as he nodded his answer, he was remembering how like her this was. Even as a girl her responsiveness and animation had been tempered by a certain mature aloofness and seriousness as subtle as her having just now turned the conversation from its lighter vein.

He wondered at the grave, serious quality in her that was so at odds with her surface prettiness, deciding that it became her, that it hinted at a depth of character to go with her looks. That she was aware of her physical attractiveness seemed apparent, for she was wearing a long, flowing riding habit of pale blue, its color accenting the lustrous coppery highlights of her hair, the whiteness of her skin, and her violet eyes. As he appreciated her costume, he also realized that good taste and her ability as a seamstress were alone responsible for it. Lola was in no position to afford such a habit unless she had made it herself.

"Your set-to with the senator has changed things, Fred," she told him now. "He's sent into town for more men. Losing Childers doesn't seem to have improved his disposition. He's offering a three-hundred-dollar reward."

"Dead or alive?" He smiled wryly as he put the question.

"Sayers didn't say. But he doesn't like the looks of it. Kirby's going too far."

"According to Sayers?"

"Yes."

He lifted his shoulders, let them fall. "Then what I came down here to see you about makes more sense." He reached out and laid a hand on the sorrel's neck. "Could I come along with you and swap this jughead for one of yours? Without," he said with an amused glint in his eyes, "your knowing anything about it?"

"Of course," she said at once, although she didn't respond to his levity. "Everyone knows by now that you're riding Lee Murchison's pet. But you can't just ride straight home with me."

"Why not?"

"This is a short cut to Summit. And the men Kirby's sending out will be coming this way." She shook her head as she saw him about to argue the point. "No, I won't let you take the chance. Tell me where you'll be tonight, and I'll have Tom bring you the best animal on the place."

He considered that a moment, giving her fears for him less thought than his plans for the night. It was late, around 5:00 he supposed, and if he went on to Cross D, he was practically doubling the miles he would have to ride to get back to the Squaw. So finally he said: "All right, Tom can do this one thing for me. But that's all. I don't want him mixed up in this."

"You may not want him but he will be," she said positively.

"We'll see," he told her, thinking a moment longer. "If he can be at The Springs tonight about nine, I'll be waiting for him."

"He'll be there. If he isn't, I will. What else can he bring?"

"Nothing, thanks. We packed plenty away from Stirrup this morning."

"Is Childers in bad shape?"

"Not too bad. But they really worked him over."

Her eyes showed a faint anger. "It was a mistake for Tom to go to Spane."

"Not his mistake. Mine, Lola."

She shrugged impatiently. "Well, someone's then. Are you leaving the country, Fred?" When he shook his head, she went on hurriedly: "Why not? There'll be nothing but trouble for you if you stay. Jim Kirby is a stubborn and powerful man."

"Hasn't he always been just that?"

She sighed at this reminder and lifted her reins, putting her horse in alongside his, her look one of real concern.

"Then be careful, Fred. By tomorrow Sayers will have every trail and every likely spot covered. He certainly knows about the cabin up Squaw."

"He can't know all the spots that'll keep a man hid."

Her expression momentarily lost its gravity and took on a trace of a smile. "Like Bady's you mean?"

The name had a familiar sound but he could connect it with nothing he remembered. "Bady's?"

"Don't you remember? The mine 'way above our place right on the side of Sentinel? You and Tom and I rode up there that autumn to fish the creek below it."

He did remember now, and, looking back over the years to find this one of the more pleasant memories, he smiled. "Sure enough. We camped there overnight, didn't we? Stuffed ourselves on trout and then had to sit up because it got so cold and we hadn't brought enough blankets. We must've made twenty trips for wood to keep that fire going."

She was pleased at his response and answered his smile, although the wistfulness of her expression told him that she was perhaps too critical in comparing those carefree days to the present. Then, when she spoke, he was sure of it, for she said: "If only we could go back to those times, Fred." She shrugged away the thought and went on. "As a matter of fact, Bady's would be about the best place I know for you to go . . . if you have to look for a place to hide. The road to it went out three or four winters ago. One of those ledges fell and wiped it out. Now the gap just hangs there two or three hundred feet up the wall of the cañon."

He frowned. "Then how would a man go about getting to Bady's?"

"From above. Tom and I just happened to find the way in last fall. I doubt that anyone else would know about it. There's nothing to take anyone up there. We wouldn't know if Tom hadn't tracked a bull elk on down from 'way above. I wonder. . . ."

"You wonder what, Lola?" he asked as she paused.

"If you could find your way in." She sat in thought a long moment, finally said: "As I remember it, we came in from the north of Sentinel, right below the peak itself. You'll find a deep notch there, the head of the cañon the road used to climb. There's a smaller rockslide there near the head of the notch, and, if we hadn't seen this elk climb it, we wouldn't have known there was a way. But there is. Once you're around the slide, you come to a ledge barely wide enough to travel. It leads you right onto the bench where we camped."

"Thanks," he drawled with a grin. "I'll keep it in mind. If they crowd me too close, there's where I'll head."

Lola looked back down the trail now in much the same way she had when they met. Then her glance swung around to him once more. "It's getting late and I'll have to go. Good luck, Fred."

"I may need it," he said as she drew on past him and went away.

He sat there, watching her go. At the top of the slope where the trail made a bend she turned briefly and looked back, then was gone. As he put his horse on down through the trees, he was wondering what kind of a man her husband had been ever to leave her.

CHAPTER THIRTEEN

Throughout the afternoon a murky gray cloud bank had been forming to the west and south, and toward sundown its shadow crept across all the low country. It touched Rita as she was turning her horse into Box's corral, the fading light heightening her look of seriousness as she thought of Tom, still wondering about him.

The cloud shadow cut short the brief twilight in the depths of Squaw Creek where Bill Childers was talking to Tom Demmler at the line shack. Tom's surprise at having found Childers there was genuine, for Spane hadn't known of the Box man's leaving Kirby. He didn't quite understand Childers being with Fred, nor did he particularly like the man being so close-mouthed about why he'd quit Kirby. For it suited his obscure involvement in this affair to have Fred very much on his own, in fact quite helpless. And he was annoyed to learn that Josh Hawks had been here earlier, and was now on his way into the hills to meet Fred. What were Fred's plans? Childers couldn't tell him a thing except that Fred wasn't on his way out. So he finally left, telling Childers he'd like to see Fred if it was at all possible for him to get over to Cross D.

The cloud shadow brought a premature darkness to the tangle of hills running northwest from the head of Stirrup's meadow. Off there in the folds of the hills lay park-like stretches of open grass dotted with the cattle Kirby had thrown onto Stirrup, and tonight a supper fire blazed brightly but out of sight in one of the deep draws near the line of the north fence.

Five men lounged around the blaze. They had finished eating but were in no hurry to start the night's work, knowing that the odds were exceedingly small that anyone would be riding this isolated corner of the range tonight to see them. Jeff Spane was one of the five.

Once, during a lull in their talk, Spane inserted a word to which they paid a strict attention. "Let the fence go once you've cut it. You can forget your back trail and make time. By sunup you ought to be above Errett's place. From there on it's a dead cinch."

The man hunkered down across the fire from Spane took a last deep drag on his smoke and tossed it into the flames, drawling: "What's the hitch? This is too easy."

"No hitch at all, Yace. Except you lose some sleep."

One of the others chuckled softly. "I could lose a damn' sight more for this kind of money. Does Marolt have everything set at his end?"

"Everything," Spane said. "But remember, fifty to sixty head is his limit. If this goes all right, we help ourselves to another bunch night after next."

"If?" It was Yace who skeptically echoed that one word. He was the shrewdest of the lot and he was eyeing Spane narrowly now. "What's Demmler taking out of this?"

Spane shrugged. "He gets a third."

"I wasn't talking about money. What else?"

"He's helping Vance clear the layout."

Yace grunted in derision. "Show me the day Demmler helps anyone but himself. He wouldn't be trying to rip Kirby up the belly, would he?"

"Hell, no," one of the others put in mildly. "He's set to marry the Kirby girl, lucky devil."

Spane had had enough of this talk and now came to his feet,

grunting against the soreness of his back and beating the dust from the seat of his pants. "I'll see you boys day after tomorrow, right here."

He had turned and started toward the horses when Yace's dry tones reminded him: "With the money."

"I'll have it."

As he left the camp and rode southeast, Spane began mulling over in his mind the implications of what Yace had said. It took a man like Yace to peg something you hadn't quite figured out yourself. As Yace had broadly hinted, Demmler must be in this for more than the money involved, even though his share was to be considerable if things developed as they should. Spane's experience with Demmler in the past had no parallel to this. Until now he had simply been one of the many who would ignore the law if it stood in the way of survival, and Spane had helped him ignore it. The Cross D had had some hard times since old Demmler's day, and a man couldn't be blamed for selling a head or two of his neighbor's beef now and then just to get along.

But this was different. This was rustling on a big scale. Furthermore, Box had over the years made a reputation for dealing with rustlers in an absolute and merciless way. If Demmler hadn't pointed out that Kirby was too busy with Vance to discover his loss until it was too late, Spane wouldn't have risked being caught with so much as a pair of wire clippers in his saddlebags. As it was, he was keeping strictly away from the actual handling of the stolen beef. He would deal directly with Marolt, handle the money, nothing else.

What about Tom Demmler? What was he after? *Why should you care?* came the immediate answer to those questions. He was getting his, and that was as far as he should interest himself.

It took him better than an hour and a half to ride out the wide circle of the upper hills and come down through the trees on Cross D. In his wary way he reined in and sat, listening, when the outline of the corral stood out of the obscurity.

He finally saw Demmler, leaning there against the gatepost, and only then walked his horse on in.

Tom heard him coming and wheeled around. He let Spane get within a few feet before asking querulously: "Where to hell you been? I've got things to do."

"You said after dark," came Spane's mild answer.

"This is two hours after dark." Tom put down his irritation then, asking: "How did it go?"

"Fine. They were all there. By now they'll have made the gather and be through the wire."

"You fixed it with Marolt?"

Spane nodded, looking down narrowly. One thing he'd had on his mind today while making that long ride across to Marolt's was to try and argue Demmler into taking a quarter share rather than a third. But now his argument didn't seem so strong and he decided to let it go as he said: "Thirty dollars a head was his limit."

"Good enough," came Tom's surprising answer. "They'll take 'em through by way of Red Rock?"

Again Spane's head tilted in the affirmative. "Clear to the head of it before they make the swing west. Even a hound wouldn't stand a prayer of following the rest of the way."

Tom's satisfied smile showed even in the starlight. "By the way, Jeff," he drawled, "they've put a reward out for Vance."

Spane peered down at him in silence a moment, trying to make out his expression. "Meaning I should try to collect it? I thought he was a friend of yours."

"He is."

Spane was able to read no meaning whatsoever into these enigmatic words and now, remembering the many miles he had to cover tonight getting back to Summit, he was suddenly impatient to be gone and asked: "When do I see you again?"

"Tomorrow night. Here, only earlier. Make it right after dark."

"We go ahead with the second batch?"

"We do."

Spane said—"OK."—and reined his horse away.

Tom stood, watching him go, wondering what contrariness in him had made him nearly tip his hand to the man. He shouldn't have mentioned the reward. He was going to have to be more careful, he was thinking, as he opened the corral gate and led out the bay and the leggy brown he had decided to take across to Fred.

He led the animals on over to the yard path, dropped the reins, and went on to the porch. He was halfway up the steps when suddenly he halted, seeing the pale gray of Lola's figure outlined against the door's black rectangle.

A sudden apprehension struck through him, and in his confusion he said with more sharpness than he intended: "What are you doing out here, Sis?"

"Trying to enjoy the night. Why, don't I belong here?"

He should have let it go at that. Instead, he gave in to his curiosity. He had to know how long she had been here, what she had seen. "That coyote was prowling around the hen house again," he said. "So I waited around, hoping for a chance at him."

"In that case you should have taken along the rifle."

Her subtly barbed words and the indolent way she leaned there against the door frame, arms folded across her breasts, goaded him into saying: "Do I have to answer to you for everything I do?"

"No one said you had to, Thomas."

He would have gone inside but for having to pass so close to her. Now he decided he wouldn't need the sheepskin he'd been on the way in to get. He turned back down the steps, keenly aware of her and irrationally resenting her presence, telling himself he didn't give one damn what she had seen.

She let him go three strides down the path before she said: "Tom, I told you Fred was through with Spane."

He stopped, wheeled slowly around. "So you did."

Now that he was sure she knew something he was instantly on the defensive.

"He was here for orders," he said. "I told him he was through. He didn't like it much."

"You're sure that's what you told him?"

"What are you trying to say, Lola?" he bridled.

At first he didn't think she was going to answer. But then in a voice toneless with scorn she breathed: "I'm saying that you're betraying Fred. I don't know how or why. But that's what I think."

A sudden fury hit him, made him burst out: "This hasn't one damned thing to do with Fred!"

"Hasn't it? Then I suppose it has to do with Kirby."

Her quiet, knowing words warned him against giving away too much. "Can I keep Spane from helping himself while Kirby's back is turned?"

She was a long moment saying: "So you're still working off the old grudge."

He knew then that she saw far deeper into him than he had realized, perhaps than he did himself. All at once he was uncertain, feeling a strange need of her understanding. "Look, Lola," he said pleadingly, "Fred would say this was right. Anything that whittles Kirby down is helping Fred."

"Not if it's done behind Fred's back. And have you forgotten Rita?"

"Leave her out of this."

"You can't leave her out of it." She stood, looking down at his shadowy shape seeming so solid there in the darkness, wishing his nature could measure up to his stature. She was suddenly pitying him, longing to help him. "Tom," she said softly, "why must you always take the easiest way?"

"I don't see what you're getting at."

"Nor do I see what you are. Whatever it is, it will only hurt you in the end."

He turned his back to her and took two impatient strides away from the porch. Then he stopped and looked around. "How else can a man like me get anything except by taking it? Tell me. How can he?"

"Tom, I. . . ."

She sensed then how impossible it was to reason with him, and her sigh of helplessness and bafflement was eloquent as she said lifelessly: "You'd better go. Fred's probably already there."

She turned then and went inside. Once across the threshold a forlorn hope stopped her and she stood with hands tightly clenched, listening. For many seconds the sound she waited for didn't come. Then abruptly Tom's boots grated against the gravelly path and for the instant that she thought he was coming toward the porch the hope in her strengthened. But then the slur of his steps faded. He had gone down the path and her hope died and she crossed the room and sank wearily onto the settee, lying back and trying not to think.

Yet thoughts would come no matter how she fought to banish them, and, when she caught the sudden hoof pound of Tom's horse going away at a hard run, she could imagine his frame of mind, the fury and the restlessness and the feeling of guilt he was trying to leave behind by outrunning them, by punishing his horse. And in the depths of her despair she faced the bitter certainty that her intuition out there had been a right one. He was betraying Fred, Rita. Worse than that, he was betraying himself.

Something underhanded and treacherous lay behind his association with Spane, yet the realization of this brought no panic in her, no surprise even. Spane was a rustler, so in her groping for an understanding of what Tom's dealings with him might be she could reach only one conclusion. Spane was stealing cattle from Kirby, the cattle Box had thrown onto Stirrup. For hadn't Tom said that what he was doing wouldn't be hurting Fred?

She could follow the confusing maze of his actions that far but no farther. At first she suspected him of some far-sighted but nevertheless futile intrigue. Yet, beyond the immediate goal of running off Kirby's cattle, she saw no ultimate one Tom could be heading for that didn't involve too many improbabilities. He had nothing but the ranch here and the lease. . . .

The lease! All at once a startling thought struck her. Tom was short of money for stocking the lease. Instead of struggling through two or three years of depending on the normal increase of his small herd adequately to stock the new range he might be making this gamble with Spane for the money that would let him buy the culls from the reservation herd. Only last night he'd been talking about that. She clearly remembered the enigmatic smile he had given when she asked where he would find the money. He had spoken casually of going to the bank and, little as she understood financial matters, she had accepted that as a possibility.

Now, as she lay there, a vast wave of relief swept over her. The tension and the nerve strain left her so completely that she felt drowsy, her mind almost at peace. There was a moment's uneasiness over so calmly accepting Tom's dishonest act. But compared to other awesome possibilities she had vaguely feared without being able to name them, his deceit and underhandedness as she saw it now seemed petty, almost trivial.

She was honest enough with herself to admit that she couldn't regret anything Kirby might lose in this. The seeds of animosity and bitterness implanted in childhood by her father had become too deeply rooted to be grubbed out completely by her mature judgment of these later years. Let Kirby have his losses. It didn't matter to her.

Tom's weakness did trouble her. But that was something she lived with perpetually, a thing that she had to make compensations for day in and day out. So she could only hope that whatever he was doing with Spane wouldn't get him into any real trouble.

With her mind at ease, or comparatively so, she thought of going on into her room and to bed. But it was pleasant, just to lie here. She reached up finally and pulled the blanket from the back of the settee, covering herself. Then she was almost at once asleep.

Long afterward Lola's deep, dreamless slumber was disturbed by the lamp's bright glow, and she turned over and away from the glare.

"Time for bed, Sis. It's past two."

She came half awake at the sound of Tom's voice, lifting a hand to shade her eyes as she looked up at him. He was smiling good-naturedly, and even though sleep dulled her thoughts she sensed the oddity of his manner compared to what it had been earlier.

She sat up, yawning and stretching. "I was so comfortable."

He sat beside her and reached over to take her chin in his hand and tilt her head so that he could look into her eyes. "The damnedest thing's just happened," he said abruptly.

His look was so eager, so excitedly secretive that it roused her completely. She remembered and asked: "Did you meet Fred?"

He nodded. "Gave him the brown and turned Murchison's nag loose. Sis, are you awake enough to listen to something?"

"Of course."

He couldn't keep the excitement from showing in his dark eyes as he said: "It's something big. Bigger than anything that's ever happened to us."

She waited for him to go on, trying to hide her misgivings. Then he told her: "Fred's selling us The Springs range!"

"I don't understand."

"He's selling, not leasing." He took her hand and squeezed it so tightly that it hurt as he went on: "It was his idea. You could've knocked me over with a broom straw. He needs money to build up his herd. He can't go to the bank for it, so I go instead. With a deed on seven thousand acres in our name, yours and mine. Imagine. The thing the old man fought for all his life is handed us on a platter!"

She was having a hard time taking this all in. She looked at him carefully, trying to read some deception in his expression. But his straightforward look was without guile and gradually she caught some of his excitement until it made her say: "Tom, it just can't be."

"I know. It's hard even for me to believe."

He went to the table to turn down the smoking wick of the lamp. Facing her again, his eyes were bright with eagerness. "Here's the way we work it. Tomorrow in town I go to Blanding or Russell, anyone but Keely. Whichever it is gets the legal description of the land and draws up the deed. I take it to Fred to sign, then record it. Next, the bank loans me every dollar the deed's worth. Half that money I turn over to Fred as a beginning payment. Or rather I take it down onto the reservation and spend it on those culls for him, along with my half. So we're both. . . ."

"It is the truth, isn't it?" she interrupted incredulously.

"Gospel, Sis." He held up a hand. "I swear it."

"Then this . . . then you're through with Spane?"

His expression changed subtly for an instant before he smiled and said in a hearty way: "Forget Spane, Lola. This other's the thing we've been waiting for ever since the day they drove us into these hills."

"I know, Tom. But. . . ."

"But nothing. Sis, we can hold up our heads now."

"I never held mine any other way," Lola said quietly.

Seeing his face at once harden in the way she knew so well, she impulsively leaned over and kissed him on the cheek. "I didn't mean that the way it sounded. I'm glad for you, Tom. It really is wonderful." She saw that she had taken the sting from her words and asked: "What about Fred? Where is he?"

"Right where he belongs. While he was with me, Childers and Hawks were across, cutting wire along the west fence. By now the three of 'em are moving all the cattle they can gather right back onto Box."

"And you didn't stay to help?"

"I tried to. Argued my arm off. But Fred wouldn't listen."

"It's best this way, Tom. You're better off away from his trouble."

He sobered. "That's something I don't get. He ropes Hawks and Childers into this, leaves me out."

"But he's not leaving you out of it. He's counting on you more than he is on them. Besides, you'll be seeing him."

"Don't think I won't." He laughed in a way that puzzled her. "Tomorrow I meet him right under Kirby's nose. Within two miles of Box. Remember that ridge to the west of Box where Kirby cut all those ties to sell the railroad?"

"You mean he's going to be there to . . . ?"

He nodded, grinning broadly. "Right there. Kirby and Sayers'll be up in the hills, so where could you find a better place? Not that I'd have thought of it."

As they went on talking, Lola caught some of his enthusiasm once more, and later, when they went to their rooms, she had the feeling that things might not be as bad for Tom as she had supposed.

CHAPTER FOURTEEN

With most of the sky covered solidly it was like moving about inside a capped barrel. Except for the infrequent intervals when there was a break and a few stars shone through Foster could see little. He was riding alone, just cruising the fence. He guessed it must be close to midnight.

There was no telling how he sensed it, but all at once he knew that there wasn't anything between the fence posts. Hardly had he recovered from his surprise when his gelding walked into a tangle of barbed wire and started crow-hopping and pitching and he had all he could do to keep from being thrown. While he was fighting to steady the animal and get him over his fright, two steers walked up out of the obscurity and straight through the fence behind him.

Foster got out of there in a hurry, down off the slope and away from the fence. Once out of sight of it he pulled in, wary and undecided as to what to do. Red Durns, his partner tonight, was at least a couple of miles farther on north and headed in the opposite direction; they had met back there about half an hour ago. It was chilly enough so that Red might have traveled even farther than two miles, jogging instead of walking his horse just to keep warm.

One thing Foster did know was that the layout was about three miles distant, that Jim Kirby was there, and that whatever he decided with Red's help would involve letting the boss know what had happened. So he rode on south, not wasting any time now that his mind was made up. In slightly more than thirty minutes he was running up the lane toward the house.

He was saved the bother of going inside, for, as he was leaving the gelding at the yard fence, a lamp came on in the living room and a few seconds later the door opened on big Jim Kirby. He had pulled on a pair of pants over his nightgown and his gray hair was rumpled, giving him a quarrelsome look even before he sighted Foster and came to the wide porch's edge to snap: "What's gone wrong?"

Foster began telling him. But Kirby didn't wait to hear it all, shortly interrupting with a brusque: "Finish it later. Get me something to ride." He was on his way in the door as he spoke.

Knowing how Kirby rode when he was in a hurry to get anywhere, Foster saddled himself a fresh animal at the corral, along with the senator's black. He had barely tightened the cinches before Kirby was there with him, saying impatiently: "Come on, man! We don't have all night for this."

The senator was carrying a double-barreled Greener twelve gauge and now took the carbine from his scabbard and leaned it against the outside of the gatepost. Nothing was said as they mounted and started away. Nothing had to be said. Jim Kirby was in a killing mood. He rode with his free hand wrapped around the shotgun's grip, steadying it in the now too short sheath. He rode exactly the way Foster had thought he would, as fast as his big chesty black could run. If it hadn't been for the cloud mass overhead breaking and letting a few stars through to relieve the blackness, Kirby might have killed his horse right there, or killed himself running into something.

They reached the point along the fence, where Foster had discovered the cut wire, in exactly half the time it had taken Foster to ride from it to headquarters, their animals badly winded and mouths foaming. Kirby had his look at the tangle of wire, at several more cattle drifting through the fence. It took him maybe ten seconds to decide something.

"Red'll be on his way back, "he said crisply. "Go get him. Find the other end of this cut and hole up near it. If you see anything in the shape of a man, shoot."

Foster made no move and after a moment Kirby said: "Well?"

"Suppose. . . ." Foster seemed to be having trouble finding the words he wanted. "I can see taking a shot at Vance, boss. But suppose we come across Bill?"

"The hell with Bill! If he's with Vance and fool enough to be caught meddling with another man's beef, then it's his lookout!"

Foster nodded and started away, thankful that Kirby had framed his order this loosely. There had been no out-and-out command that Bill was to be shot on sight and he would make a point of telling Red just that. This job was a good one, more than Foster had ever expected to get out of Box, but it wasn't good enough to keep him here if it meant throwing lead at a man like Bill Childers.

Kirby let Foster get out of sight before putting the black on through to the Stirrup side of the fence. Now that he was here and actually seeing what Vance had had the gall to do, his fury subsided somewhat, to be replaced by a cold and calculating resentment. He was struck by the fact that with all his money, a big crew, and the weight of the law behind him, one man had single-handedly thrown his life so out of balance that he was neglecting all his other affairs in the face of this personal feud.

He thought back over the years, trying to remember a comparable situation. Not since he had been a young man had he let any one individual disrupt the broad pattern of his life to the point of driving him personally to physical violence. And the fact that John Vance had been that individual he now took as something of an omen. He had long ago convinced himself that he had been in the right in his difference with the elder

Vance and the same brand of stubborn reasoning told him he was in the right now as far as the younger one was concerned. Whatever doubts he had, he was refusing to recognize.

Foster's mention of Childers had touched closely on one of those doubts, for losing his foreman had made a deep impression on Jim Kirby. He wasn't dead sure that Childers was with Vance, but if that were the case, he would dismiss any feeling for Childers in the same way he ruled out the notion that Vance was within his rights in moving Box's herd off Stirrup. Milt Hurd's signature was on the lease, Vance was wanted for killing Hurd, and until that legal tangle was unknotted one way or the other he was going to protect his interests.

Now that he was out here, shivering a little against the chill air and actually hunting a man, he was gripped for a moment by a feeling of impotence. *How the hell do I find him?* about summed up his attitude as he walked the black on in and out of sight of the fence. At that point he really put his mind to the problem.

Sooner or later Vance and whoever was with him would be riding close to the fence. Or would they? For a moment he tried to reason as Vance would, and in that way he got his answer. Knowing that Box might have fence riders out, the logical thing for Vance to do would be to cut the fence and then keep away from it, working the cattle toward it from deep inside Stirrup range and letting them simply drift through.

Once that notion struck him, Kirby stopped and sat, listening. Presently he heard a steer bawl far to his left. He turned that way. He had ridden only two hundred yards when he came upon four animals plodding in the direction of the break. He put the black in the opposite direction.

He was lifting the Greener from under his leg when he began wondering about the black being gun-shy. He thought back, trying to remember if he'd ever shot from the back of this particular animal. In the end he decided he hadn't and, shrugging aside this doubtful factor, broke the shotgun open and dropped in two brass-bound shells. He had made certain back there at the house to bring along only buckshot loads.

As he rode slowly on, he passed more cattle, a pair, several single animals, then a bunch of five that shied out of his way and lumbered off into the dark. His glance became restless, and once he lifted the Greener with a sudden motion and lined it at a black outline coming up out of the shadows, a form he took to be that of a man on a horse. But it was nothing but an oddly shaped cedar and he let his breath out in a gusty sigh of disappointment and went on, the Greener cradled across his rein arm.

He had gone on for about five more minutes when suddenly a sound turned him rigid. It was a man's voice close ahead, cursing lazily, good-naturedly. The next instant he heard the voice again from obliquely to his right. Then the indistinct outlines of a bunch of cattle moved up out of the darkness, followed by that of a tall rider swinging a rope end at the rump of a laggard steer.

Kirby swung the Greener around, knowing that this could be no one but Fred Vance. One of the closest steers saw him and wheeled away as he was drawing back the shotgun's two hammers. He saw Vance catch the steer's motion and turn his head his way. He lifted the Greener into line as Vance's horse came to an abrupt halt. Then his fingers were closing on the triggers.

Long afterward when he could look back on the moment dispassionately, Jim Kirby was to wonder exactly what impulse made him lighten the pressure of his fingers on the triggers for that barest fraction of a second.

For one thing the darkness made it hard to see the end of the barrels and be sure of his target. For another, he was suddenly struck by the awesomeness of the thing he was about to do, shoot a man down in cold blood.

But then, as he saw Vance's shape melt toward the ground from the saddle, he lined the Greener quickly and fired one barrel. He was afterward to wonder, also, if his memory served him right in telling him he had aimed well above the empty saddle.

It all happened too quickly to be sure of anything, of the instinct that guided him either before or after the weapon's pounding blast. But that his black reared suddenly and viciously was a certainty. So was the answering thunder of Vance's Colt, along with the shudder that ran through the black as the animal's forelegs hit the ground and buckled.

Involuntarily Kirby threw himself sideways from the wounded horse. He lit hard on one shoulder, and by the time he had scrambled clear of his animal's flailing hoofs and was on his feet again, Vance was a blurred, hunched-over shadow on the back of his horse going away at a hard run.

Kirby brought the Greener up then and let go with the other barrel, knowing full well that the range was too great for the buckshot to more than sting whatever flesh it hit, horse's or man's. Vance faded from his sight and he stood listening to the rhythmic, fading hoof mutter of the man's horse going away, his hands trembling as he reloaded the Greener and put a shot through the black's head.

He was turning away when a voice close by said: "Jim, don't move!"

It was Childers. He had a carbine slanted across the horn of the saddle, and as he walked his horse in out of the shadows, Kirby was thinking of the load left in the Greener, wondering if he could beat Childers to the shot. He was suddenly boiling with indignation at what had happened.

Childers stopped a few feet short of him. "I saw the last of it," he drawled. His right hand lifted from the carbine and fell against it with a soft slapping sound. "If you'd hit him, you'd be where the jughead is now."

Kirby said nothing, held speechless by his anger.

"You're on Vance's land. Get off!"

There was an uncompromising ring in Childers's voice that brought back Kirby's reason now. He saw at once that Childers was even more furious than he. And, knowing how much it took to crowd the man to that point, he was warned to be very careful now.

He slowly lifted the shotgun and let it hang from the bend of his arm. He wanted to say something but didn't know what it was. For a moment he considered taking his saddle from the dead horse and lugging it back to the fence. In the end he decided against it.

He turned then, quite humbly, and strode away.

Childers, as Kirby faded from sight, sighed a deep sigh and moved his hand up to let the carbine's hammer off cock. He had been in dead earnest.

CHAPTER FIFTEEN

Toward dawn the clouds that had been piling against the peaks all night cooled and began shedding some of their moisture. It was a misty rain at first but gradually strengthened to a steady downpour. It brought the sheriff's posse from their blankets high along the Summit road and gathered them about a feeble fire and a pot of coffee until day's wan gray light thinned the blackness. They one and all decided to forget breakfast for an hour, long enough to ride to Box. They were unanimous even to Ben Sayers in blaming their discomfort on big Jim Kirby, and they were expecting a real meal when they finally turned their horses into Box's corral and walked on up to the crew wing of the house.

They did get a real meal—steaks and eggs, fried potatoes, canned corn, tomatoes, and griddlecakes, plenty of strong black coffee. They were halfway finished when Kirby himself came in and sat down at table with them, saying a sober: " 'Morning, boys." He looked tired and glum.

All but Ben Sayers hurried through the meal and got out with Foster and Red Durns in the wagon shed, where they soon learned the reason for the senator's bad mood. Meanwhile, back at the table, Sayers was nicely judging the moment for saying something he'd had on his mind all night. He let Jim Kirby empty his plate and get well into his second cup of coffee before coming out with it.

"Well, Jim, this rain spoils something I had in mind to do today."

Kirby looked across at him morosely, making no comment, so Sayers cleared his throat and went on: "Porter and Abe were up Squaw yesterday, looking over that line shack. No one was there, not even Hawks. They found sign, plenty of it. But it didn't mean much. Last night when they mentioned it, I was reminded of something."

"What?"

"Before Vance got away, he claimed it would be easy to go up there and find his tracks and Hawks's. The ones they made coming down to Stirrup the night Milt cashed in."

Kirby sat straighter, seeming more like himself. "You mean you didn't have a man check that?"

"No. Between looking after Vance and listening to you and Keely argue the thing, I couldn't get away. Like I say, I was going up there today."

Kirby's look was pleased. "So now Vance's chance there is washed out. Can you think of any other chance he has?"

"Only Hawks."

"Who's going to believe anything Hawks has to say?" Kirby's hand lifted in a deprecating gesture.

Sayers eyed the senator with a knowing smile, saying unexpectedly: "You don't think Vance did it any more than I do, Jim."

"The hell I don't!" Kirby blustered, avoiding the lawman's amused glance. "He had the reason. He had the chance."

"And he doesn't have it in him."

Kirby's jaw muscles stood out suddenly. "Ben," he said tonelessly, "let me remind you you've got a warrant to serve. Anything you may think privately hasn't a damned thing to do with your official responsibilities."

"I know that, so don't get your dander up. I'll go through the motions. But try and find anyone else who will. This bunch of mine's headed for town right now. They're through. They're as smart as you and I. They've made up their minds Vance isn't guilty and. . . ."

"And you can jail every last one of them if they refuse to serve as deputies."

"All right, I lock 'em up. Then what?"

"Get some others."

"Where? You tried that yesterday. Everyone was busy." When Kirby made no reply, only sat glaring at him, Sayers added: "The word'll get around, Jim. You keep pushing this and you'll lose more votes than you can win back in a month's campaigning." Still Kirby didn't speak and shortly the lawman continued: "Pretty soon they'll be saying you're using your office to make a land grab. Think where you'll be then."

Kirby stood up and went to the front window, turning his back on the sheriff and staring out into the rain. The silence ran on for many seconds until finally he said: "Then I'll make a trade with you, Ben. Find me the man that put the bullet through Milt Hurd and you can light a cigar with Vance's warrant."

"And meantime?"

"Meantime I go to the papers tomorrow with a statement. In that statement I. . . ."

"You'll make it hard for me."

Kirby turned his head and stared back over his shoulder. "I'll give the facts, which are these. In the public interest I'm insisting that Vance be brought to trial. I admit there are some doubts as to his guilt. But I still demand that the law do something about a calculated murder."

Sayers let out his breath in a tired, defeated way. "That's what I said. You'll make it hard for me. And easier on yourself."

Kirby's eyes showed amusement, though his expression

remained serious. "Ben, a politician always leaves himself a way out of a tight spot. You've been at the game long enough to know that."

"So I have." Sayers lifted his thick bulk erect. "Maybe I've been at it too long."

He went to the door and paused to look around. But Kirby's back was turned again, so he merely lifted his heavy shoulders sparely, took his poncho from the chair, and left.

After he had gone, Kirby moved over to the door and stood looking out through its glass upper half. He watched Sayers and the other townsmen plodding down through the drizzle to the corral. He kept eyeing them until they had saddled and started out the lane. Then, without thinking, he started to lift his right hand to his face. The sudden stab of pain in his shoulder made him grunt and hunch forward with a sharp intake of breath.

He cursed irritably, profanely, and went out and along the porch to the main part of the house. Crossing the big living room on the way to his office, he caught the slam of a door at the end of the bedroom wing and idly wondered what could be taking Rita outside at this early hour.

Had he been curious enough to go see, he would have found her hesitating there by the door, wearing an old curl-brim Stetson, a poncho, and, for the second straight day, Joe Banks's waist overalls. After debating something for several seconds, she stepped out into the rain and walked on around to the back of the house, beyond that skirting the root cellar and chicken yard and presently going into the barn by its door that faced away from the house.

In the barn she climbed to the loft, found a pitchfork, and with it waded to the open loft door overlooking the corral. Glancing down, she saw that three horses were there, her paint gelding one of them. They stood with heads down, rumps turned to the slant of the rain.

She pitched a forkful of hay out the door, and then climbed back down to get a bridle. Outside again, she climbed through the back poles of the corral, easily caught the feeding paint, and got the bridle on him. She made a second trip into the barn for saddle and blanket and had some difficulty lifting them to the corral's top pole. But finally she had the paint saddled and ready and knew that to this moment her father couldn't possibly have seen her.

There was but one way out of the corral and the gate lay in plain sight of Jim Kirby's office window. So she wasted no time leading the paint out, closing the gate, and getting into the saddle. She rode on around the corral until the barn was again between her and the house before she turned away toward the open country. Only when she was far enough away for the trees to be nothing but blurred shadows beyond the shroud of the misty rain did she breathe easily with a feeling she was safe. Then, angling slightly toward the north, she let the paint steady down to a tireless jog. She was taking the shortest route she knew to the foot of Squaw Cañon.

She had eaten breakfast in the kitchen, listening to Charley Samuels, the overworked cook, complain about having to get six extra meals on the table. Foster had come in for a sack of grub to take across to the men still at Stirrup and from him she had learned of last night, of her father's encounter with Vance and Bill Childers. Putting this news alongside Foster's hunch that Sayers's posse men were disgusted and returning to town, she had rightly concluded that Jim Kirby would be in a bad frame of mind this morning. She had no intention of letting him drag her into another argument about his troubles.

So, deciding to get away from the house, she had suddenly made up her mind to go through with something she had last night lain awake thinking about. That something had to do with Fred Vance. Until this moment her idea of finding Fred and talking to him had seemed a perfectly logical thing. But now she understood that she was probably going through the discomfort of this long ride for nothing. Sayers and his posse hadn't found a trace of him and it wasn't at all likely that she could, either.

She supposed that Tom might be able to help her. But she had a strange feeling about Tom. After trying every way she knew to excuse him and explain his lie of yesterday, she had finally been forced to the conclusion that he must be somehow really involved with Spane. That shocked her. She would never be quite at ease with him again until her vague but nevertheless real suspicion of him was gone.

Last night when her faith in him had weakened and then broken completely, there had been a strange absence of any emotion but sadness tinged with pity for him. At first it was irritating to think that her regard for him couldn't withstand such a test; she began wondering if she was lacking in feeling. But then the real truth came to her. The fact was that she simply liked Tom, that love didn't enter into their relations, never had. Perhaps her wanting to see him have the chances that had been denied his father had made her take him too seriously. At any rate, she had proved herself mistaken in thinking him the one man she cared for above all others.

Now, realizing finally how slim were her chances of finding Fred, she almost turned back. What finally sent her on was a belief in the right of the thing she had decided last night—that and a particularly acute dread of having to discuss this affair any further with her father. She had the whole day before her, she liked riding in the rain, and there was that barest chance that she might be able to reach Fred.

CHAPTER SIXTEEN

Rita found Josh Hawks at the line shack up Squaw Creek, alone. Out of politeness he asked her in. He had a fire in the stove, and, while she stood by it, warming her hands, he put on coffee. She decided at once against any casual talk and bluntly told him the purpose of her visit.

His comment was: "Fred? I thought they had him locked up."

"They did." She studied his expression, trying to see beneath its blandness. But the old wolfer had a pokerface and it made her angry to think she couldn't read it. So she said pleadingly: "Josh, you've got maybe a dozen reasons for thinking I'm from the wrong side of the fence. But you also think a lot of Fred Vance. You've got to believe I'm only trying to help him."

He lifted his hands, palms outward, and his look became contrite. "Miss Kirby, I got nothing in the world against you. But you might as well ask me to turn off the rain as to take you to Fred when. . . ."

"When you thought he was locked up," she cut in dryly, helplessly. She thought a moment and her glance was trying to stare him down. "You're anything but stupid, Josh. You've been roaming these hills the last couple days. If you haven't been wearing a blindfold, you've seen a lot of strange riders."

He frowned. "Now that you mention it, I did come across a couple up. . . ."

"Yes. And you can save yourself telling me you wondered

what they were doing. You know as well as I do what's been going on. Sayers has been hunting Vance and hasn't found him. Bill Childers is with Vance and nothing could please me more. You've been with him yourself, or I've got two Chinese uncles. Now will you stop treating me like a child and take me to him?"

Hawks's innocent look abruptly faded and he couldn't repress a chuckle, for her voice had risen and she was a pretty picture standing there with cheeks aglow and her eyes afire.

"You can blindfold me if you want," she insisted. "But I've got to find him. Today!"

Hawks scratched his head, eyeing her amusedly. "Y'know, miss, Bill was saying only last night that you could be a holy terror if someone crossed you. Like your father. I begin to see it."

"I'm not like my father! And even if I am, what's wrong with that?"

Nothing." Hawks reached for his hat and poncho and, as he put them on, looked around at her to ask: "You want to go now or do we wait for that coffee?"

"Now."

Her intentness sobered him and without a further word he went on out and up to the brush corral for his horse. Some minutes later as they headed down the cañon together, he admitted worriedly: "We may miss him altogether if he's seen Demmler."

"What about Tom?"

Hawks gave her a wary glance and said guardedly: "They had something to talk over."

That made her curious, but not to the point of asking him anything further. She had what she wanted now, or was soon to have it, and that was enough.

From the foot of the cañon Hawks struck out through the lower hills in a direction that almost exactly backtracked Rita's way in, and after they had gone on that way for some twenty minutes she asked: "You aren't taking me home, are you?"

"Mighty close to it."

She had to be satisfied with that answer and in something under an hour was finding out how accurate it had been. For, even though the rain held on, they passed close enough to Box for her to imagine she could see the house as a low-lying shadow to the south. Then, farther on, Hawks came to the washed-out ruts of the old tie camp road and followed them on toward the timbered ridge she often watched change color in the sunsets from her northwest bedroom window. She suspected then where they were to find Fred Vance, and the audacity of his being this close to Box awed her.

Presently, up in the lodgepoles back from the face of the ridge, they skirted the remains of the sawdust pile and Hawks led the way into the timber. They came abruptly upon a lean-to built of scrub oak and cedar. A fire burned in front of the makeshift shelter. It was comparatively dry there and as Hawks told her—"Far as we go, miss."—she stopped the paint and sat listening to the sibilant whisper of the rain brushing the tops of the pines, wondering what their next move was to be.

Although no one was in sight, Hawks ground-haltered his horse and walked over to the fire saying: "He'll want to look us over."

She was on edge as she joined him, a nervous anticipation gripping her. She gave a start as a branch snapped, the sound coming from close behind her. Turning, she saw Fred Vance striding toward them.

He was carrying a rifle and a voluminous rain-streaked poncho robbed him of some of his tallness. His face looked drawn, tired, and she was suddenly gripped by a strange emotion, a blend of admiration for this man and a deep anger toward her father for what he was doing.

As Vance came in on the fire, Hawks told him: "I always was an easy mark for a woman, Fred. She talked me into this."

Vance nodded, leaning the Winchester against a pole inside the shelter. "You've got a nice camp here, Josh," he said as he unbuckled the slicker and laid it aside. He was eyeing Rita politely, but with an alive, unmistakable interest as he added: "It's a bad day to be out, Miss Kirby."

"I had to see you," Rita said quietly. "And I did talk Josh into it."

"Doesn't matter. Only you may have to stay longer than you want. Someone's meeting me here and I can't let you go till after that."

She nodded. "I know. It's Tom. Was he helping you last night?"

"Not at the time you're thinking of. We met earlier."

She was keenly disappointed, at the same time realizing the contrariness of feeling this way about Tom. His not having helped his friend at a time when that help was surely needed shouldn't interest her in the slightest. Nevertheless, she was thinking that Bill Childers had been with Vance last night and his acquaintance with the man didn't begin to approach Tom's long-standing friendship with him.

Now as she thought once more of her errand, her glance went uncertainly to Hawks. He pretended not to notice but in another moment ambled on over to his horse, saying: "There's a trap I lost up above last winter. Now's a good time to look for it."

Vance, having intercepted her glance and noticed Hawks's reaction to it, waited until the wolfer had ridden out of earshot before drawling: "Maybe I ought to call him back. Maybe I'll need a witness to this, whatever it's going to be."

Only when she read the amused look in his eyes did she realize he wasn't serious. And then, all at once uneasy about her being here and having to know what his answer would be, she told him bluntly with a rush of words: "I came about the lease. You've said you don't want one. But I thought this might be different. I'd like to run my own herd on Stirrup without Dad having a thing to do with it. I'd even put up a bond that cattle of his never came inside your fence."

His eyes had opened wider as she spoke and now he started to say something. But her fear that she hadn't carried her point made her quickly put in: "Don't say no till you've thought it over, Fred." She hesitated uneasily, shortly adding: "That was a slip. But I was with Tom yesterday. We talked about you and he never calls you Vance."

"The Fred suits me fine," he said. "It's the rest I don't get. Where does this herd of yours come from? From your . . . ?"

"Not from Dad," she interrupted, knowing what he was going to say. "Josh should be able to tell you that I run my own brand. It'll be my own money, too, whatever you charge me. We needn't even call it a lease. Call it a simple grazing fee. And forget that my name's Kirby. I might be anyone, just any rancher making you an honest offer."

"But you aren't just anyone."

The solemn framing of his words, the way he was regarding her now with such a suddenly awakened and direct interest, brought her an awesome and powerful awareness of him physically. In the depths of her being there rose an emotion the like of which she had never before experienced. It was an awakening, almost a rejoicing in being here with him, in being able to read into the quiet look of his blue eyes a response that was somehow reserved for her alone.

She heard herself saying: "You're trying to say something. What is it?"

"What is it?" He shrugged, yet his glance held her steadily, and when he spoke again it was almost angrily: "You're Jim Kirby's daughter and still I listen to you. It would be hard refusing you anything."

"Then forget I'm a woman."

He shook his head. "Has Tom ever told you how downright.
. . ." He broke off his words with a visible restraint and the
deeply probing glance he had fixed on her changed before a
meager smile. She knew that she had seen the last of that
unguarded emotion in him before he drawled: "You haven't
finished your offer. What would it be?"

It took her a moment to think back. "Five dollars the head
from now until shipping time in October."

He considered that a moment, finally saying: "Five wouldn't
be enough."

"Then six, seven. Whatever's fair. I'll leave it to you to set the
figure."

"What I meant was that it wouldn't be enough to change my
mind on a lease. I just plain don't want one."

"But it's money in your pocket."

"So was your father's offer."

She was groping for a further argument as she said: "You
won't see a dollar of Dad's money until he's sure of Stirrup. You
could have mine tomorrow."

This seemed to impress him, for he asked: "How many head
would you want to throw in there?"

"A hundred to start with. More later, if we can round them
up and herd them."

"The layout can graze ten times that many, Rita."

"Then I'll buy more." Her hopes were coming alive again
and she thought of something that made her say urgently: "If it
turns out that you're able to be back on Stirrup, you can't hope
to build up your herd in just one summer. Use the graze money
to buy more cattle. We'd be on the place together on a . . . call
it a temporary partnership."

"And if I don't get back on Stirrup?"

"Then I'd bank the money for you. Or send it wherever you are." She turned then at a sound, seeing Hawks on his way in through the trees. "Or Josh could take charge of it."

As Hawks came up now, Vance looked his way with an abrupt grin. "She's got a better business head than her father, Josh."

"Which is possible," came the wolfer's dour opinion.

Vance laughed softly at the look she gave Hawks, saying: "You'd be in hot water with your father."

"I'll risk that."

He sobered at some thought, drawling: "You'd more likely be Tom's partner than mine. Which is as it should be."

She was unaccountably annoyed at his inference, yet managed to keep her feelings hidden. "I'd thought of his lease. We could get along."

"You haven't seen him since last night?" He waited for her shake of the head to add: "Then you can't know that I'm selling him everything east of The Springs, not leasing it."

She was so surprised, even so unaccountably disturbed by what he said, that it took her a long moment to remember that she should pretend to be delighted. "How fine for him. And for Lola."

"Fine for me, too." A slight frown betrayed his puzzlement over her lack of enthusiasm. "Thanks to the two of you, I should have a good backlog for making a fresh start."

So casually had he spoken that she almost missed the expected meaning of his words. And now she breathed excitedly: "Then you take my offer?"

She liked his smile, the way his eyes once more showed that strong awareness of her as he said: "Yes. We should hit it off better than your father and I do."

She was all at once overjoyed, yet feeling a sudden let-down. She wanted to thank him yet couldn't think of a way of doing it and could only hope that he understood.

He evidently did, for he said now: "No use in your staying until Tom gets here. Josh will take you back down."

Here was more proof of his trust in her. She was humble in the face of it and wanted to say or do something that would show him how grateful she was. So on an impulse she told him: "Sayers took his men back to town this morning, which could mean anything or nothing. But I'm having a talk with Dad when I get back. Is there anything you can tell me that'll help?"

"Help how?"

"To persuade him to give up the lease, to forget that warrant."

"You could tell him I'm signing an agreement with you, that after it's signed his lease with Milt's signature won't be worth anything."

"I've already thought of that. There's nothing else?"

"Tell him if he strings that wire again, it's coming right down."

She couldn't help smiling at that as she shook her head. "I'm afraid that wouldn't make much of an impression. But I'll think of something."

She walked out to the paint now, reaching up to brush the rain from the saddle. When she had climbed astride it, she looked across at him. "I won't try to thank you, Fred. Is there some place I can meet you tomorrow? I'll have the papers with me and maybe, just maybe, some better news about Dad."

"Why not here, if Sayers has pulled in his horns?"

"It may be he hasn't. I'd rather you didn't take the chance."

"Then wherever you say."

She tried to think of a place that would be safe for him if Sayers did change his mind. Finally she remembered one. "Do you know the homestead above The Springs?"

"Dean's old place? Yes."

"There, then."

She waited for his nod, and then turned the paint away. As

she rode out through the trees, the rain beginning to pelt her shoulders more strongly, she was struck by the thought: *If Tom could only be like that.* For a moment she was sobered by the change one single day had brought in her outlook. She had lost faith in the one man who had over the past months really interested her, and she had found a much firmer faith in another who was hardly more than a stranger.

Fred Vance stayed in her thoughts as she followed the road down through the timber along the face of the ridge, and then out across the rolling, treeless sweep of land backing Box's headquarters. She was honest enough with herself to admit more than a passing interest in him. Once, when the prospect of his being at Stirrup after his troubles were over came to her, she felt an odd, pleasurable anticipation.

Without realizing it, she began wondering how she was going to break the news to her father that she had decided never to spend another winter in Washington. Then, knowing that she had never before reached the point of giving this ultimatum, that her thoughts of Fred Vance alone had prompted it, she felt a strong embarrassment and knew that she would have to think up a better reason. But her mind was made up. She wasn't going to live in the East beyond the summer.

When she rode in past the side of the house and turned along the yard fence, it was to see Jim Kirby, hitching a team to the buggy down by the wagon shed. He saw her coming, finished fastening a throatlatch on the nearest animal, and turned and waited.

"Going to town," he said as she approached. "Want to come along?"

Earlier she would have wanted nothing less than to make the drive to Lodgepole with him. But now she said at once: "Yes. Give me time to change."

"Where've you been?"

She crowded back the mischievous impulse to tell him the truth, remembering that Fred would still be there on the ridge, waiting for Tom. Instead, she told him: "Enjoying the rain."

He shook his head. "You've got some queer ideas, girl. But come along if you want. You may be coming home alone unless you'd like to stay the night. I've got some wires to get off and answers to wait for."

She gave him her horse to turn into the corral and hurried up to the house. They drove away from the yard gate ten minutes later and hadn't gone a mile before Rita realized that he was in unusually good spirits.

"What's happened, Dad? After last night you should be tearing your hair."

He gave her a quick glance that was briefly angry, then amused. "So I should. But I'm glad it turned out the way· it did."

"Glad?" she echoed incredulously.

He nodded. "Suppose it turns out someone else killed Hurd? How would I feel if I'd put that buckshot through Vance?"

"Dad," she breathed, "you can't be in your right mind."

"I am. Furthermore, what happens to Vance is up to Sayers from now on."

"You mean . . . ?"

"I mean it's up to the county to investigate a murder."

"And you're giving up the lease?"

"No. I'll go to court with that just as I've planned." She smiled in such a knowing way that he said brusquely: "Laugh if you want, but I'm within my rights and I'll damn' well get what's coming to me."

"You're wrong, Dad. You're not within your rights."

"How would you know?"

"Because," she said, "I'm moving onto Stirrup myself. Under an agreement signed by Fred Vance, not Milt Hurd." She went on to tell him about it.

Only once did he manage to recover from his surprise enough to ask: "How in the name of heaven did you find him girl?"

"That's the one thing I can't tell you," she answered, and told him the rest.

CHAPTER SEVENTEEN

Tom Demmler left the Lodgepole road two miles below Box and circled the ranch headquarters, keeping well out of sight of it. The rain was easing off and, by the time he swung back to the abandoned tie road and started following it on toward the ridge, the drizzle had broken so that it came only occasionally in light misty flurries, while off to the west the clouds were breaking and showed patches of bright blue sky. There was a freshness and a greenness to everything that suited Tom's mood, for last night's talk with Fred Vance had purged his mind of a lot of uncertainty and pettiness, and today he felt himself a bigger and a stronger man secured by a foundation of integrity that, regardless of its source, was a new and pleasant thing.

Fred Vance was waiting where last night he had said he would be. Finding Josh Hawks also present was something of a surprise. So was what they had to tell Tom of last night's encounter with Kirby, of Rita's visit this morning, and of her plan for meeting Fred at Dean's clearing tomorrow.

Tom was unaccountably disappointed over this new development but managed to hide his feelings well. They talked about Rita for several minutes before Fred asked to see the deed. Along with it Tom produced a carefully wrapped bottle of ink and a pen, and Fred signed the paper after giving it only a cursory glance.

"Don't you even read it over?" Tom wanted to know.

"Why?" Vance drawled casually. "You think this lawyer,

Russell, is all right or you wouldn't have gone to him. So why spend time trying to make sense of all these two-dollar words?"

Tom shrugged and said: "Suit yourself." He put the deed in his jumper pocket, adding: "Only I'd be more careful if I was doing it. Just the same as I'd think twice about this offer Rita's making."

Vance eyed his friend in puzzlement. "That's a queer thing for the man who's marrying her to say."

Tom felt his face flushing but kept doggedly on, leading up to the thing he had in mind—something he'd given a great deal of thought to last night and this morning. "All right, I'll pull in my horns. Rita's fine. But I don't trust Jim Kirby, that's all. Maybe it's a hang-over from the old days."

Something he said piqued Vance's curiosity. "What's her proposition got to do with her father? He didn't even know she'd come up here."

"Probably not. Certainly not if she said so. But look at this from Kirby's end, Fred."

"I'm trying to." Vance's frown deepened. He waited a moment and, when Tom didn't speak, drawled: "Maybe you'd better help me."

Tom appeared hesitant, trying to find a way of expressing himself. "My hunch is . . . is that Kirby'll let her go ahead with it. Why? Because he's keeping Stirrup in the family." He lifted a hand as Vance started to interrupt, continuing: "Of course he doesn't have Stirrup in any legal sense. But suppose something happens to you?"

"Like what?"

"Like what almost happened last night. He's been trying to make it happen, hasn't he?"

Vance tilted his head. "Go on."

"If it did happen, Stirrup would be put up for sale, wouldn't it? You don't have anyone to hand it down to. And who stands

148

the best chance of getting it? The lease holder, Kirby."

"Rita, you mean."

"Kirby or Rita, they're one and the same. Another thing. Who in this country could swing that big a deal, buying an outfit the size of Stirrup? Just Kirby, no one else. If anyone could bid against him, it would be some cattle outfit from outside. But there's Kirby already on your layout with a grazing permit . . . or rather a member of his family. Because of that, he'd have a say on whoever bought it. But can you see the sheriff, or the courts, or whoever manages the sale, favoring an outsider over Kirby? No. He'd name his own price, and there he'd be with Stirrup. Finally, after all these years of trying, he'd have it."

Vance's look had gradually changed. The glance he had fixed on Tom was probing, almost wondering. "I didn't know you hated Kirby's guts this much, Tom. What happens when you're one of the family?"

"I'm marrying Rita, not her father." Tom had spoken so quietly, so gravely that Vance was impressed.

Hawks had been building a smoke and now offered his tobacco, and Vance took it to stare down vacantly at his hands as he rolled the paper around the weed. He was wholly absorbed by his thoughts, carefully deliberating everything Tom had said.

Finally he looked around obliquely at Tom with a broadening grin, drawling: "And here I've thought all along I was the only one that felt that way about our senator. I was trying to keep you clear of the mess because of. . . ."

"Because of Rita?" Tom asked dryly. "She and I have thrashed that out. I take just so much of the old man as I have to, no more." An angry expression hardened the look of his square face. "Don't forget I'm a Demmler, Fred. Twenty or thirty years ago that meant something. Ask Josh what it meant, if you can't remember yourself."

Hawks was eyeing Tom narrowly. "I know what it meant once," he said. "But that doesn't hold for now, Tom."

"Why doesn't it?" Tom retorted quickly. "I live with it every damned day of my life. It's with me every time I go to town to ask for credit, every time a blizzard hits and I break my back hauling feed to a snowed-in herd while the outfits down here let their cattle drift to where they can get their own feed. Don't tell me it doesn't hold for now."

"Then what do I do?" Vance asked gently.

"About what?" Tom had been so wholly gripped by his anger that he didn't catch Vance's meaning.

"About Kirby's chances at Stirrup if anything happens to me."

Tom drew in a deep sigh and shook his head. "Don't ask me. You're better at figuring those things than I."

"Do I draw up a will?"

Tom's face showed a wry humor. "At your age? No. But you could cut Kirby off at the pockets by giving Josh here an option to buy Stirrup. Josh Hawks or Bill Childers or Lola . . . any real friend."

"Not me!" Hawks shook his head vehemently. "I've never wanted to own any more than I could tote around with me."

"You, then?" Vance asked Tom.

"It doesn't have to be me. But it damn' well ought to be someone." Tom looked away, afraid of betraying the sudden excitement he was feeling.

"You're the best one I can think of." Vance held out a hand. "Get out your ink again and we'll write it on the back of the deed."

Slowly Tom reached to his pocket. "You're sure you want to do this? Maybe I've gone loco, friend. Maybe it's just a lot of damn' foolishness."

"Who cares whether it is or isn't?" Vance's expression

abruptly went serious. "The chance is there. Why take it? Hand it over."

So Tom took out the deed and they stepped over to Tom's bay horse while Vance used the flat skirt of the saddle to write against, pausing once to say: "I'm making the option for a year and saying it holds only in case I cash in. OK?"

"Whatever you say," Tom answered, and Vance went on with the writing.

It was later when Tom was ready to leave, already in the saddle, that he abruptly thought of something and said: "Lord, it nearly slipped my mind, Fred! But Spane's on the prod."

When Vance looked up at him quizzically, he went on: "He showed up at the layout last night saying you owed him for what he did at your place the other night. I told him to go to hell. He said he'd be back."

Vance thought a moment. "Pay him and I'll settle with you."

Tom smiled meagerly and shook his head. "Not unless I have to. But I thought you ought to know how he feels in case you ever run across him again."

Much later, after he had left the ridge and was crossing the gently rolling grasslands behind Box on his way to the eastern foothills, Tom Demmler was thankful for having said that about Spane. It was just one wiped-out track along the back trail of this double game he was playing.

There was so much for him to think about now, there were so many possibilities opening up, that it was in a way awesome to contemplate. Once he told himself: *If only Spane and I could have dragged it out longer.* But this was only rationalization. He was being dishonest with himself, for the prospect of another $600 or $700 share of Marolt's money no longer attracted him. He was contemplating a bigger thing, a possibility that dwarfed any he had ever before faced. And in his weak, opportunist way he began looking into that possibility.

That night, when Spane showed up at the corral again, they talked about it, argued even. By the time Spane left they had agreed to something.

CHAPTER EIGHTEEN

The next day was a full one for Jim Kirby. He had anticipated this yesterday afternoon when he hired a buckboard for Rita to drive home instead of waiting over until this morning. Shortly before noon the answers to his telegrams of yesterday to Washington began coming in and were brought to him one by one from the station by the station agent's youngster. Each time he'd give the boy a dime and josh him, saying something like: "Son, if you keep this up, you'll have all my money!" The boy liked it and so did Kirby.

One wire displeased him so much that he hurried on up to the station and sent off a long answer, explaining the postponement of his Washington trip, saying he planned to be on the way there two days from now and that he was definitely interested in being considered as a possibility to head the Department of the Interior.

On leaving the station he started thinking back on what Sayers had said yesterday morning. Last night's talk with the sheriff had gained him nothing but the lawman's promise that, once he'd caught up on his office work, he would try recruiting a posse and begin another hunt for Vance. Now, knowing how the town must be talking about his stubbornness where Vance was concerned, he stopped at the print shop and spent twenty minutes with Blaine Rounsville, editor of the *Clarion*. He left there convinced that this week's paper would carry an editorial praising him as a public benefactor because of his insistence that the only known suspect in the Milton Hurd murder should be apprehended.

One of his major political fences thus put in good repair, he loafed on down to Bill Yount's saloon, stopping several times on the way to pass a pleasant word with various friends and acquaintances. Letting himself be seen around town shaking the hand of homesteader or rancher or business owner or housewife alike was the kind of thing people remembered at election time.

Finally arriving at the saloon, he filled a plate at the free-lunch counter in back and took it to a nearby table. Before he had finished eating, the afternoon regulars arrived and took over the back poker layout. When Kirby left his table, it was to move to that one on their invitation.

He liked poker and alternated between a hard-bluffing game and a shrewd and canny one so that his opponents had difficulty anticipating what he'd do next, and today he was consistently winning, as most always happened. Toward the middle of the afternoon he looked up to see Tom Demmler watching the play, and he nodded to Tom, and was then reminded that Rita was expecting him home for supper.

When that hand was finished and he was raking in the dollars, half dollars, and quarters from the table's center, he observed: "Looks like I won't get home to eat unless I leave the winner."

"Stick around," one of the others said.

"Guess I'll have to," Kirby said.

The play went on, and presently Tom Demmler left for the street.

At 6:00, when they finally cashed in, Jim Kirby was winner by $18. On his way up to the hotel to eat he was telling himself that here again was something people would remember about him, his reputation for being good at cards even though he didn't play often. The voters weren't sending a hard-luck man to Washington to look after their interests.

This had been a good day. After a last call at the telegraph office to make certain there were no more messages, he stopped at the livery yard for the team and buggy, and headed out the Box road at a crisp trot, enjoying the cool darkness, feeling really at his ease for the first time since the night trip East had been called off. He was even wondering if he shouldn't pull out of Stirrup and tear up Milt Hurd's lease. As a gesture toward the son of his old enemy such a move would be long remembered.

The buggy's lamps laid a weak glow along the road's uneven surface ahead and Kirby got to watching the shadows, trying to guess by them exactly where he was along this road he knew so well. It was a game he enjoyed and often on a night drive he would test his memory this way. The rocky cut through the approach to the Elk Creek bridge was familiar even before the buggy's iron tires were rumbling against the planks. Farther on he recognized the cedars closely flanking the road along the slope below Turkey Hill.

The horses were at a slow jog when they reached the branching of the Stirrup trail off to the right. It was directly beyond this that he picked up the sharp outlines of a horse's legs standing out from the other shadows at the road's edge in the orange wash of the lamps.

His glance whipped up. A small-bodied rider sat the horse. He was quieting his nervous animal with a constant movement of his rein hand. In the other he held a carbine. The weapon was leveled slackly the senator's way.

Kirby hauled his team down to an abrupt stop. He had barely recognized Jeff Spane when Spane was saying: "Keep your hands where they are and we'll get along fine, Senator."

Kirby was conscious then of the weight of the Colt at his left armpit, though he rarely thought of the weapon. He was also feeling a nameless alarm as he tonelessly said: "I thought we'd warned you off this range, Spane."

"So you did." The rustler's head tilted sparely. His cool glance was mocking, almost amused.

"Then get off!"

"I will," Spane drawled, "when I've spoken my piece."

"Do you have to speak it down the barrel of a gun?"

"Maybe I do, Kirby. It's this. If you want your daughter back, pull out of Stirrup."

Kirby was a second or two taking in the full implication of those words. When he understood them, he sat bolt upright on the seat. "Where is Rita?"

"Vance has her."

"You lie!" Kirby said hoarsely. A stark and sudden fear struck him.

Spane nodded sparely. He backed his horse slowly off into the shadows now, saying smoothly: "Go see. Only remember, you don't get her back till every critter you own is on Box's side of that west fence!"

Kirby wasn't sure of the exact moment Spane started away. He caught the quick hoof pound of the man's horse and his fury goaded him out of his paralysis then. He stabbed his hand under his coat and brought out the Colt.

He leaned forward on the seat, cursing the way the lamps blinded him, leveling the weapon. He emptied it in a furious jabbing of his big hand and Spane, off in the darkness, swerved his horse deftly aside when the first explosion came.

Spane ran a full two hundred yards before easing his animal down to a stop. He listened and heard nothing from the direction of the road. Then from off to his left sounded a low-pitched voice asking: "How'd it go, Jeff?"

That voice belonged to Tom Demmler.

CHAPTER NINETEEN

This day had been an endless gamble for Tom Demmler, an almost constant play against long odds. It had begun this morning when, wanting to be far from the scene when Spane met Rita, he had come on into Lodgepole early. There, in the middle of the afternoon, he had seen Jim Kirby well established at Bill Yount's poker layout and by a freakish stroke of luck had overheard the senator's remark about staying in town for the evening meal.

That had been the big gamble, that hunch that he just might be able to get out to Cross D for the meeting with Spane at dark and with Spane intercept Kirby on his way home. He hadn't dreamed that this bet would pay off the way it had. And now it looked like he was winning the last gamble of all. He was back in town well ahead of Kirby, he knew, and the chances were that anyone seeing him on the street would assume he'd been here throughout the late afternoon and evening.

Best of all, Spane's end of this was working out to perfection. Between the man's feeling of resentment toward Box and his love of money he could be relied upon absolutely until tomorrow night, when he would show up at Cross D's corral for the last half of Tom's share of the Marolt money. What happened to him after that didn't interest Tom beyond the certainty that he would have to leave the country and would probably never be heard from again.

Sauntering up the dark street after having used the alley gate of the livery corral, Tom rolled a smoke and lit it with a trembling hand, for the first time realizing that he had figuratively drawn his cards, that it was too late to draw others, that he would have to play out his hand as it stood now. He didn't let his thoughts dwell too long on certain things, one of which was what this day must have meant for Rita. In fact, he was keeping his thoughts pretty much on dead center, with the instinctive knowledge that to mull over the uncertainties was pointless and would only undermine his confidence, which was at best none too firm.

He came up on the wooden awning of Yount's saloon and stood at the walk's edge just beyond the pale wash of lamplight shining through the grimy windows, the tautness of his nerves easing slowly away. He had been there perhaps three minutes when he idly noticed a feeble glow of light abruptly go out in the window of the hardware store across the way. Shortly he heard the slam of the store's door and guessed that Sidney Connover must be locking up after an evening's work. Then shortly he saw Sidney's slat-bodied shape start on down the walk.

On impulse he called: "That you, Sid?"

Connover stopped. "Who is it?" He started out across the street and halfway to the walk said: "Oh, you, Tom. Couldn't make you out."

"You work too hard, Sid," Tom drawled as the other joined him. "You need a drink as bad as I do. Doesn't anything ever go on in this town? I've been in all day and done nothing but wear out boot leather and the seat of my pants."

Sidney laughed, obviously pleased at this encounter with Lola's brother. "What would you have, grand opera and a tent show? This is a weekday."

"And a dull one." They started toward the saloon's swing doors when abruptly Tom halted, looking back downstreet as the sound of a team coming in at a hard run shuttled up to him. "Someone in a hell of a hurry," he said, and started on past Sidney who was also listening.

Sidney stayed as he was, his look worried. "Something odd about it."

They stood there, listening, as the sound strengthened. There were few lights down there but Tom shortly imagined he could see Kirby's buggy swinging in at the courthouse rail a moment before the hoof rattle suddenly broke off. He said then: "Well, do I match you for this drink?" They went on in and over to the bar.

Tom lost on their toss for drinks and this for some obscure reason nettled him, made him wonder if his luck was taking a bad turn. He was excited, tense, and, as they filled their glasses, he had to rest his arm against the bar to keep his hand from shaking. He downed the whiskey at a gulp and quickly helped himself to a second glass, thankful that Sidney didn't notice. They made small talk for several minutes, Sidney mentioning Lola once in a polite way, and it was then that Tom decided to bait the man.

"She's a funny girl," he said casually. "Moons around half the time, hardly knowing what she's doing. I think she's been hit hard."

Sidney gulped. "Some man, you mean?"

"That's the best guess I can make."

"But the last time I saw her she. . . ." Sidney's words broke off suddenly. Someone on the street had shouted stridently. He and Tom were both looking toward the doors as they burst inward and Bob Larkin, the station agent, came in. At this late hour there were only a dozen or so other men in the room and now all were eyeing the doors, the shout having taken their attention.

Larkin's appearance at once quieted the low run of talk. His look was alarmed, sober, as he stopped there holding the doors wide and saying: "Something's happened! To Jim Kirby's daughter. Sayers wants you all down at the courthouse right away!"

He started to say more, but stopped. He turned then and hurried out, obviously bound up the street to the hotel and restaurant to spread the news. The doors had barely swung shut behind him when chairs scraped at the poker layout and the men there came to their feet.

Tom looked around to find Sidney staring at him in a disbelieving, shocked way. He set his glass down, said tonelessly: "I'd better get up there."

Sidney laid a hand on his arm. "It can't be as bad as he made it sound, Tom. Don't worry."

Tom nodded and moved as two men who were about to go out stepped respectfully aside to make way for him. He was glad to be out of their sight, for he was nervous and suddenly afraid, really afraid. Larkin's manner and the way the others back there had reacted to it had brought home to him the deadly seriousness of the thing he had done. Somehow in planning this with Spane he hadn't until now let himself contemplate the fact of the awful risk he would be running.

He took his time on the way down to the courthouse, trying to get a hold on himself, knowing that the next few minutes would be the most critical of all this day. Yet when he stepped into the courthouse's gloomily lit hallway and heard the run of low voices sounding out of the sheriff's office, he was all at once calm and serious.

He went in. Sayers and Kirby, standing by the window, both looked around at him. Three other men were on the near side of the room but he didn't look their way as he went over and, his glance on Kirby, gravely said: "Larkin didn't say much. What about Rita?"

Never had he seen Jim Kirby as he was now. The man had aged considerably and he seemed not so big as usual. His face looked flabby rather than hard and there was a stunned, hurt expression in his eyes.

"She's gone," Kirby said quietly. "Vance has her. He's holding her till I've moved off his place."

"Vance?" Tom shook his head. "I don't believe it."

Instead of the angry rejoinder Kirby would normally have made he said simply: "It's so, Tom."

Sayers put in: "Spane stopped Jim on his way home about an hour ago. Vance had sent him."

"How do you know it was Vance? Maybe that's what Spane said," Tom insisted stubbornly with a good show of anger. "But it can't be! I saw Fred two days ago. We signed a deed. . . ."

"We know all that," the lawman cut in tonelessly. "But there's no question about this. Spane was there at Stirrup the other night and moved Jim's crew . . . hell, you know what happened as well as I do. Vance had sent him."

"Spane can say he's working for Fred and still not be. The other night there at his place he pulled Spane off Childers and ran him out."

"A put-up job if I ever saw one."

"Put up how?"

"Supposing a no-account like Spane worked for you," Sayers said. "You'd try and let on like he didn't, wouldn't you? I'll admit Vance had me fooled. But he's using Spane and this time he's gone too far. Men have been strung up for laying hands on a woman. We're out to get him."

Sayers's hard-to-rouse temper was really on edge. Now Jim Kirby said tiredly: "You can argue it any way you want, but I'm not going to let you send these men out, Ben. If anything would happen to Rita, I'd. . . ."

"Nothing'll happen to her. When Vance sees he can't get

away with this, he'll turn her loose."

Kirby sighed. "I can't stop you, of course. But that herd is coming off the lease. Beginning tonight, as soon as I can get back to my ranch."

Steps sounded along the hallway and two more men came into the room, one of them asking: "How many of us can you use, Sheriff?"

As Sayers started talking, Kirby took Tom by the arm and led him out into the hall.

Sayers saw them on the way out and called: "You hang around, Tom!"

When they were several steps from the door, Kirby stopped, eyeing Tom soberly. "You've got to help me."

"I will. Any way I can."

"Find Vance. Just that. Tell him I'm forgetting the lease and moving out."

Tom frowned. "That's a big order. How do I . . . ?"

"Rita told me yesterday you'd seen him. If you found him once, you can do it again."

"Not now. I don't believe all this yet," Tom said grimly. "But if he really did this, he's no longer any friend of mine."

"Still, you know where he's been hanging out. All I ask is for you to try to find him."

"I'll do that anyway." As an afterthought Tom let his right hand lightly lift the holster at his thigh.

Kirby saw that. "All I care about is Rita, Tom. Just remember that. Right now I can't think of anything but that I caused it all."

Just then Sayers came to his door and called loudly—"Everyone inside here!"—and the men waiting in the hallway, plus three more coming in off the street, filed on into the office. As Kirby and Tom came in the door, Kirby said in a low voice: "Remember, I'm counting on you, Tom. She means a lot to both of us." And with a parting lift of the hand, he went down the steps and out onto the street.

Tom edged his way into Sayers's crowded office and pulled the door shut behind him. The click of the latch was a signal that quieted the low mutter of conversation and centered all attention on the sheriff, who stood by his desk.

For a long moment Sayers's glance studied the faces before him—there were sixteen, according to his count. At length he drew in a deep breath and said gruffly: "Now that the senator's gone we can get down to cases. Ideas are a dime a dozen around here right now. A few of you doubt that Vance had a hand in this. But once you're sworn in you're bound to do your duty as peace officers the same as me. Here's what your orders are to be. You'll take this runt, Jeff Spane, any way you can. I won't complain if he's a job for the coroner. As to Vance, you'll try and take him without using your guns. But if you're crowded into it, you'll treat him just as you do Spane. I want him. Everyone get that?"

There were some whispers and one or two voices rose in angry undertones. Over those sounds the lawman called: "Anyone that can't fill the bill is free to pull out now!"

Two men near the back wall turned and made their way to the door, one of them saying loudly enough for the rest to hear: "No son of John Vance would ever lay hands on a woman, by God!" The others watched the speaker and his companion go out, making no comment, eyeing them soberly and with a faint antagonism.

The door had barely swung shut when Sayers looked at Tom, asking: "What about you, Demmler?"

"I stay."

"Remember, once you take the oath you're the same as the next man."

Tom's face was ruddier than usual and his look was angry as

he drawled: "If Vance is guilty, I'll be rougher on him than you will, Ben. But I hope he isn't. I don't believe he is. That's what I think and it's up to you on whether or not you use me."

Sayers regarded him solemnly for several seconds, a tense silence holding the others. Then finally the lawman said: "All right, I use you. I'm giving you Mel Boynton, Bill Hill, and Charley Ames, and you'll work that country above your place as far north as the head of Squaw Creek. There you'll tie in with my men working the country to both sides of the pass. You can settle it between you how to go about it, but I want you high up in those hills by the time it's light enough to see." His glance shifted to one of the others. "Yount, you'll put your men south as far as the reservation. I want every trail covered, every likely hide-out looked at. Each man's to bring along blankets, grub for three days, and a spare horse. Now lift your right hands and say what I say after me." And he read the oath of office and made them deputies.

There was more talk, sober talk about meeting places, trails to be covered, and as the low hum of voices filled the room, Tom made his arrangements with Hill, Boynton, and Ames. It was agreed finally that they would be at Tom's place at 3:30 in the morning so as to allow them time enough to be well toward the peaks by sunup.

The crowd began dispersing, and Tom made his way out into the hall, anxious to be away from there now. Outside, as he was going down the steps to the street door, a man called after him: "What d'you think of your sidekick now, Tom?"

He answered solemnly: "We'll see, Ralph."

He was glad to be alone and hurried on up the street toward the livery yard, thinking that only one more important detail remained undone. He had to find Fred and warn him. He would try the line shack up the Squaw first of all.

CHAPTER TWENTY

At about the time Tom Demmler was leaving town after the meeting in the sheriff's office, Fred Vance was wading his horse across Squaw Creek and riding up to the line shack. He had barely pulled in close to the shack and was coming aground when Josh Hawks and Bill Childers came toward him out of the shadows, the wolfer saying querulously: "It's about time! I thought we were going down there for another night's work. Where you . . . ?"

Just then Bill struck a match to light a smoke and by its light Hawks caught the bleak, hard set of Vance's face and cut off his words, not finishing what he had been about to say but quickly asking: "Something gone wrong?"

Vance nodded soberly. "I'm afraid so." For a moment he stood eyeing them gravely, his granite-like expression not softening. Then as Bill's match died out, he dropped the reins and began talking in a furious, toneless way.

They hadn't seen him since early morning, so he told them how he had gone to Dean's clearing at midday to meet Rita. She hadn't been there; she wasn't there an hour later. Not particularly concerned about her, thinking she had possibly changed her mind about her plan for grazing Stirrup, he had nevertheless been curious enough to follow the trail she would have ridden on southwest from the clearing. The trail was unmarked, washed clean by yesterday's rain.

A mile below the homestead he had suddenly come upon

sign, tracks he assumed were those of her horse along with those of another animal that had lined up out of the timber to cut hers off. There had been the unmistakable signs of a struggle clearly readable along the trail. Someone—and at first he thought it was a Box rider Kirby had sent to follow his daughter—had stopped Rita by using force. Both horses had then struck north into the higher hills. Vance had followed the sign all afternoon until dark, finally ruling out the guess that the man with Rita had been sent by Kirby, for he was taking Rita in a direction opposite to the one that would have led back to Box.

He had finally lost the sign along a deep rocky ravine several miles above Squaw Creek. After dark he had spent three hours circling the head of it, hoping even then that he might hear or see something, a fire perhaps, that would give him some inkling of what had happened to the girl.

"So," he ended by saying, "that's all I know." He squatted on his heels, took a match from shirt pocket, and smoothed a patch of ground close in front of him, drawling: "Let's have a light."

Bill Childers struck another match, his swollen and bruised face bearing a solemn, worried look as, along with Hawks, he kneeled close beside Vance. Gouging the dark topsoil, Vance painstakingly drew a pattern that gradually took on the shape of on oversize horseshoe. Its shape was peculiar, bowed out notice-ably at one side with the cleat at the back sharply curved in.

Bill had lit his third match when Vance finally rocked back on his heels and, looking at Hawks, asked: "Mean anything?"

Hawks immediately nodded. "Sure it does."

"What?"

Hawks came slowly erect, glancing at Bill in a faintly alarmed way as he said: "You're not going to like this, Fred."

"Go on," Hawks said flatly.

The old wolfer sighed. "It was three or four days ago I ran across that same track up above. You know how it is with me," he said uneasily. "I keep a pretty close tally on who wanders around up here. Thinks I . . . 'Some jasper on his way through taking a short cut from the pass to town.' But then early yesterday I cut the same sign again up in the timber where the trees grew too close to let the rain through. So I started following it . . . you know, just curious. Well, damned if it didn't wind up right at Tom Demmler's corral."

Vance's head lifted quickly. Before he could say anything, Hawks hurried on: "Lola was there, and I stopped to pass the time o' day with her. She didn't know about any strangers having been around the place. So I come back here and pulled in just in time to be a welcoming committee for the Kirby girl when she. . . ."

"Spane," Vance breathed, rising to his feet. "Don't you remember what Tom told us yesterday about Spane?"

Hawks nodded, noticing even in the starlight the worried set of Vance's lean face. "So it's that little sidewinder that's got her," the wolfer said, low-voiced.

Abruptly Vance moved on past him and into the shack. Hawks looked at Bill, shaking his head, and afterward they followed Vance on in. He was lighting a lamp, and as soon as it was burning, he went to the stove and, taking a pie tin from the shelf above it, helped himself to some of the still warm stew sitting at the stove's back edge.

As Vance started eating, Hawks said lamely: "Look, son. About Tom. I didn't mean to let on that he. . . ."

He seemed to run out of words and a moment afterward Vance was saying: "I know. Tom hates Spane just as bad as we do. Maybe he can help us. Maybe he'd know where to look for Spane." His glance shifted abruptly to Bill. "Think you could get across to Box and pick up anything?"

For a moment Bill's look was a trifle uncertain. But then he said solemnly: "I can try." And without further ceremony he took his hat from a nail over the bunks and started for the door.

"Josh'll be here, waiting for you," Vance said as Bill went out.

"And where'll you be?" the wolfer asked after the door had closed.

"Seeing Tom. He ought to know about this. Then I'll meet you two later up where I lost the sign. We want to be on the move as soon as it's light enough to read the ground."

In ten more minutes Vance was in the saddle again, his bedroll tied to the cantle, headed downcañon. It took him forty minutes to reach Cross D, and as he rode down through the timber toward the Demmlers' cabin, the fear he had kept deep inside himself broke loose and he was as close to panic as he had ever been at the thought of Rita in Jeff Spane's hands.

He came around behind the cabin and knocked on the back door. Getting no answer, he walked on around to the front and rapped on the window of the room he remembered was Tom's. Slowly he faced the disappointment of the cabin's being empty and went back and tried the kitchen door, and found it open.

Inside, by the flare of a match, he could see no sign of recent occupancy. There were no dishes on the table. But a piece of paper and a pencil lay there. Only the hope that it might tell him of Tom's whereabouts made him stop and read it. It was a note Lola had written at midafternoon. All it said was: *Am spending the night with Mildred Anderson. Back sometime in the morning.*

Had he known where Anderson lived, he would have ridden on and tried to find Lola. As it was, he rode away from the cabin feeling let down and more worried than ever. He was heading back for the ravine where he had lost Rita's sign.

The position of the stars told him it was well past midnight when he came to the foot of the ravine. He had carefully described to Josh the place where he had lost the tracks in the maze of rubble and talus filling the ravine bottom and now he came down out of the saddle on a grassy bench directly above that point.

He was strongly tempted to build a fire, because of the night chill and since he wasn't at all sure that Josh knew exactly where the spot was. But the possibility that Spane might be camped nearby, that a blaze would warn him away, finally made him decide to wait it out in the dark.

Some forty minutes after he had taken off the saddle and staked out the brown, he caught sounds echoing up faintly from the foot of the slope and knew that someone was climbing toward him. He reached for the Winchester and stood with it cradled in his arm until presently he made out the indistinct shapes of two riders coming slowly up along the bush-dotted slope below. In several more seconds he recognized Hawks's spare shape, then Bill Childers's, and called to them.

Hawks was swinging stiffly aground when he said with typical bluntness: "Fella, you're in a bad spot. Tell him, Bill."

Childers spoke reluctantly, as though in telling of what he had learned at Box he was himself guilty of placing the indictment Kirby's crew had spoken against Fred Vance. Hardly had he finished his story when Josh added to it. While Josh was waiting at the line shack for Bill, Tom Demmler had come in with the news of the posse and Sayers's plans for the morning. "He wanted to come up here with us," the wolfer said. "But I told him he'd be helping us more if he'd keep his men clear of this country so we'd have a chance to run down Spane. So that's what he's doing."

Long after he had finished speaking, he and Bill watched Vance pacing back and forth before the spot where their bedrolls lay. Once Vance halted abruptly, saying: "Just what was it Tom said about Spane?"

"That he saw him last night there at his corral again. That he had paid him off for you. Twenty dollars. That he said he'd push his teeth in if he ever showed up at the layout again."

"And yet Lola didn't know about it when you saw her yesterday?"

Hawks shook his head. "Now that you mention it, that does seem queer."

"Why queer?" Vance said at once, a fierce loyalty toward Tom Demmler rising out of the tangle of his thoughts. "I got him into this mess with Spane and he probably thinks Lola wouldn't understand. After all, a man doesn't own up to dealings with Spane's kind unless he has to. So don't take it out on Tom."

"Who said I was taking it out on him?" After these querulous words the wolfer asked: "Well, what do we do? You want to turn yourself in to Sayers and prove to him you didn't have a hand in what's happened to the girl?"

"No," Vance said quietly. "I stay here. But you two are heading for Summit. You'll wait up there for Sayers."

"Why?" It was Bill who put the question.

"Because if you stick with me, they'll be hunting you."

"And who the hell cares if they do?" Bill asked flatly.

"I do. Before you know it you'll. . . ."

"Son, sometimes you remind me of your old man," Hawks cut in. "He'd now and then take a whole load on his back and want no help. I'd like a dollar for every time I told him what Bill's just told you. We're up here, maybe mighty close to where Spane is. And you can't shake us. So why waste your wind talking nonsense?" As he finished speaking, Hawks reached for his bedroll and started unlacing it.

Vance knew it was useless to protest further. So he said only: "Thanks, both of you." And he followed Hawks's example and unrolled his blankets.

Several minutes later, after they had turned in, he spoke to them again. "Then when it's light enough, we start looking. Josh, you'll work on up this side of the cut with Bill across from you. I'll go on and swing a circle up above. If one of us cuts the sign, he can waste a couple of shells letting the other two know. Can you think of anything else?"

"Only that I could use some sleep," Hawks said.

Long after he could hear the wolfer and Bill breathing evenly in their sleep, Vance lay awake, staring up at the brightly winking stars, thinking of Rita. His sampling of Jeff Spane's brutality there at Stirrup the other night suggested possibilities now that were too frightening to let his imagination dwell upon them. So he tried to think of Rita as she had been yesterday near the tie camp on the ridge behind Box.

Those minutes with her had let him glimpse strong and mysterious undercurrents running beneath the surface of her striking loveliness. Here was a woman who could be all things to a man, whose spirit and sensitivity would be forever refreshing, whose nature would have such countless facets that a lifetime with her would be a wondrous and never-the-same experience. He could summon a dozen clear images of her, could remember her mannerisms so vividly that it was as though they had only just now parted. There was the way her dark eyes betrayed a smile before its coming. Her voice had such a richness and expressiveness that it often gave her words a secondary meaning. She seemed incapable of any physical awkwardness and her femininity was subtle yet compelling.

Understanding for the first time now how really powerfully she had stirred him only filled Vance with a sense of guilt, and abruptly he was struck by the futility of his thoughts of her. Remembering that she belonged to Tom, or soon would, brought on a loneliness in him that was vast and overpowering. For the first time since his coming to Lodgepole he experienced a deep-rooted doubt over what he had set out to do.

Finally, mercifully sleep washed out the troubled run of his thoughts.

CHAPTER TWENTY-ONE

Sheriff Ben Sayers was as deadly serious in this manhunt as he had been half-hearted about the earlier one. He didn't leave his office until well past 11:00, and, when he did finally blow out the lamp and trudge wearily out of the courthouse, it was to get into the saddle and begin the long ride to the pass road with fourteen other townsmen.

He was worried, really concerned. Furthermore he was uncertain, which was a rare state of mind for him. He usually prided himself on being able to judge men, and the fact of his having judged Fred Vance so wrongly was a galling thing. Typically he had set out to correct that error and try to make amends. He was taking Rita's disappearance as a personal responsibility.

As the horses jogged along, steadily climbing toward the forks of the Summit road, he made a careful summing up of the things he had done to anticipate Vance's moves. First of all Carson, the best man at reading sign in this end of the territory, was to be at Box at dawn to see if he could pick up Rita's trail and follow it. Sayers fervently hoped that Carson would have some luck. For the marked change this trouble had made in Jim Kirby, aside from the fact that Box's crew was probably already at Stirrup beginning the work of pushing the cattle out, had more than anything else driven home to the lawman the seriousness of this thing.

The placing of his posse men had taken some careful thought.

He'd had to make his guesses on where Spane and Vance might be holed up and act accordingly, not overlooking the fact that he might be wrong. So he had decided to concentrate on that vast sweep of mountainous country stretching southward from Summit to a line directly east of town, where the hills started falling away toward the reservation flats. Just to play it safe, he was even watching that southern flank.

Bill Yount was in charge of six men down there in the south. They were spread thinly, having a twenty-mile stretch of rough country to watch, but they would call on the reservation police for help, and Sayers felt he had done the best he could at that end. Joining Yount to the north would be Tom Demmler with his three men. And still farther to the north would be his own main body working the hills to either side of Summit and the pass.

Ben Sayers had a certain idea about Summit, which was the reason, after they had ridden for three hours, that he stopped his men a mile below the settlement and spoke to them seriously for several minutes. Thereafter they split two ways from the road and, threading through the blackness of the aspen forest as they climbed, quietly surrounded the dreary town. Then, four pairs of men working with lanterns, they proceeded to rout out the twenty-odd inhabitants and go through each building down to the last boarded-up shanty. Sidney Connover even took three men back into the timber and searched the ruin of the old sawmill camp.

They discovered nothing. If the dour and sullen collection of shady characters they questioned even knew Spane or Vance, they wouldn't admit it.

Finally, when the posse had gathered in the vacant lot below what was once Summit's general store, Sayers told each man which stretch of country he was to ride. Every man would be in the saddle till 10:00 this morning, at which time half would come to this camp to rest until 4:00 in the afternoon, at which time they would go out as a relief to those who had been riding all day. Signals were agreed on—three shots would mean either Vance or Spane, or both, had been sighted; two would indicate that likely sign had been found. Sayers himself would be riding where his fancy took him. He was going south to begin with, to make sure that Demmler had his men where they should be.

The sheriff started out with the others at ten minutes past 4:00.

At about that time, with the first faint grayness tingeing the sky, Tom Demmler was climbing his bay horse fast through the maze of the higher hills some miles to the south of Summit. Ames, Boynton, and Hill were spread out to the south in that order. Tom had purposely picked this northernmost stretch of country to ride, for the cañon Josh Hawks had mentioned last night, the one where Fred had lost Spane's sign, lay up there. Tom was now almost even with the head of it, having remembered a vantage point well above from which he hoped to be able to look out over most of its length at first light.

There was a furtiveness about the way he traveled—he was keeping the hill crests between himself and the line of the ravine, picking rocky going when he could find it—and had anyone asked him why he rode in this manner, he would have been hard put to account for it. Why he had even chosen to come up here was another intangible. He did have some vague notion of possibly seeing Childers or Hawks or even Vance. If he met Hawks or Childers, he would let them know where it was safe for Vance to ride. If he met Vance himself—well, circumstances would govern what he was to do. He didn't have anything particular in mind, or wouldn't admit to himself that he had.

Now as the light strengthened he became impatient and used the spur on the bay over the last quarter mile that finally sent him riding up on the broad base of a high pinnacle rock. From here he could see far downward and the ravine was in sight as he had hoped it would be, the pattern of its twisting course already faintly discernible in the thinning blackness. He looked behind him, toward what should have been higher ground, and was unaccountably relieved to find the ground rocky and falling away instead of climbing.

This was important and he sat there a good half minute studying the terrain. This high rock finger jutted from the downslope edge of a trough that ran a gradually descending course along the side of the mountain. The depression deepened as it swung southward and, though the light was poor, Tom decided that a black patch perhaps half a mile down along its course must be a stand of timber. At that point the trough ran in behind a hill fold. Its outer parapet varied in height but, he judged, was at most places high enough to hide a man on horseback from view of anyone below.

He led the bay on down to the bottom of the depression some thirty feet away and wound the reins about a small jutting ledge. Climbing back to the base of the rock finger, he found a bench-like shelf where he could sit without silhouetting himself, and, as he began his vigil, he was suddenly hungry for the taste of tobacco but wouldn't give in to that craving. There was a strange, bleak emptiness in him that defied his understanding, yet he wouldn't probe his thoughts too deeply to find the reason for it.

The light was still poor. He could barely make out the shapes of individual trees down the slope that ran unevenly to the head of the ravine nearly a mile away. Its depths were still in heavy, mysterious shadow.

He had been sitting there for perhaps five minutes when all at once his eye caught a hint of movement below. Over the next ten seconds he studied the spot without seeing what had moved.

Then abruptly a speckled pattern stood out against the dark background barely a hundred yards below and he made out the shape of a fawn standing head high, alerted. The next moment a doe close to the fawn wheeled away and into precipitate flight, the fawn following. Briefly he watched their bounding, wary run before his glance swung back to find the reason for it.

Now another shadowy shape was moving out from the blackness of the trees below the spot where they had been standing. He gradually made out the shape as a man on horseback. The animal was at a slow walk. The rider made a high shape in the saddle even though he was hunched forward and appeared to be studying the ground. He was perhaps three hundred yards away. Slowly, certainly the conviction came that it could be no one but Fred Vance.

Tom Demmler's move then was impulsive, headlong. He ran on down to the bay and pulled the carbine from its sheath on the saddle. He levered a shell into the weapon's chamber, softly, slowly; his hands were trembling. He was short of breath.

Cat-footing on back into the deep shadow behind the high rock pinnacle, he took off his hat and laid it aside. And then for the first time over this brief interval he gave conscious thought to what he was doing.

It hauled him up short, awed, frightened. Across his mind's eye, typically, there flashed a kaleidoscopic and tantalizing series of images, none of which he paused to consider any longer than it took to fit it to his scheme of things. He saw a defeated and humbled Jim Kirby moving crew and cattle from Stirrup in panicked haste. He saw all that vast, rich range abandoned and waiting for the fulfillment of what Fred had written on the deed day before yesterday. He saw the sorry layout where they had driven his father to be locked in by the fastness of the hills. And he saw Fred Vance's indistinct shape climbing slowly toward him.

Go on! a wild and reckless voice cried from deep in his being. *It's yours for the taking!*

Deliberately he laid the rifle in line, the hammer cocked. But then, as his finger tightened on the trigger, he saw Vance turn away downslope again, and in that instant he realized that two other forces were lessening his chances. The light was so poor that the front sight was a fuzzy blur in the notch of the rear and the range was long, around two hundred yards, at the limit of the .30-30's effective range.

A cold sweat was breaking out across his brow as he summoned all the hunter's cunning that was in him. He took a coarser aim, lifting the front sight in the buckhorn notch because he was aiming downward. Then he let out half a breath and squeezed with his whole hand.

The carbine's flat explosion came before he was ready. He saw Vance's animal rear awkwardly, saw Vance falling sideways from the saddle, pulling his rifle from the boot. He levered in another shell and aimed at Vance and fired, instinct alone guiding him. Hard on the heel of the weapon's explosion he heard the buzzing drones of his bullet ricocheting. Vance was on his feet, the carbine in hand and running downslope. His horse was down, thrashing.

From deep within Tom Demmler there rose a cold fury at seeing his quarry escaping. He deliberately aimed at Vance's back, fired. Vance suddenly lost balance and fell in a rolling sprawl and a surge of hope ran through Tom.

But then Vance came to his knees, swinging around, rocking the carbine squarely into line with Tom's spot. A sudden panic hit Tom and he threw himself back out of sight. He was still in motion when a shard of rock rattled down off the shelf where he had been sitting a moment ago, followed instantly by the crack of Vance's rifle.

He lunged erect, snatched up his hat, and ran down to the

bay. He tore the reins loose and wasted a second climbing to the saddle because he had the rifle in hand. He viciously jerked the reins, and, as the bay lunged to a run down along the rocky trough, he somehow managed to get the rifle in its boot.

There were several places where the trough shallowed and there he bent low along the bay's neck, afraid that even in this poor light he might be recognized. When he finally reached the lower fringe of aspens in safety, his relief was so vast and overwhelming that he felt suddenly weak, weary to the bone.

He stopped there where the trees hid him, looking back. The distance was great and only by locating the rock finger did he finally see Vance's faint shape climbing the slope toward his downed animal. Then, from far below, he caught the rapid mutter of hoof echoes and knew that either Childers or Hawks must be on their way up to Vance. He got out of there then, going fast.

That crouching, shadowy figure having slid out of his sight a fraction of a second before he fired, Fred Vance lunged erect and started running up the slope, catching his breath at a sharp stab of pain in his side. He had taken but a dozen strides when a hoof clatter from above told him that Spane—for he reasoned it could be no one but Spane—was getting away.

He stood there, breathing hard, hunched over and favoring his right side, the black anger in him slowly subsiding. His glance followed the sound of the retreating horse and once he briefly glimpsed the rider as a dark, hunched-over shadow moving swiftly across a break in that upward parapet of rock. Then, the hoof falls gradually fading downward toward a rim of timber, he plodded wearily on up to the brown. From below now he caught the strengthening pound of another horse on the run and coming toward him.

He supposed it must be Josh Hawks. It really didn't matter. Nothing mattered except that he'd had his chance at Spane and had lost it. He looked down at the brown, dead now, and turned away with a deep sigh of disgust. Then the cool wetness along his side made him look down there for the first time.

His jumper was already darkly stained, and, when he pulled it aside, it was to see a bigger patch of crimson on his shirt just above the belt. When he pulled out the tail of his shirt, the cool air hit the wound and made it smart painfully. The bullet had left a deep three-inch channel in the flesh along the line of his bottom rib. The bone had evidently turned the lead, which had lost its drive because of the distance it had traveled.

When Hawks ran his horse hard up the slope, a minute later, Vance was sitting by the brown, holding a bandanna to the wound. The old wolfer pulled his heaving horse to a stand close by, saw the blood, and breathed: "Good God, I thought they'd got you. Who was it?"

"Spane." Vance's head tilted toward the rock finger above. "He was up there. He could be a better shot."

Hawks swung aground and dropped the reins, kneeling alongside, his expression a worried one. He pulled Vance's hand aside and saw the ugly wound. "Not much better. You mean to say he . . . ?"

He cut his words short as a distant crashing sound, much like a rider pushing his way through brush might make, shuttled across from along the slope toward the north.

"Bill," Vance said.

But Hawks shook his head. "If it's Bill, someone's with him." His glance became alarmed. "You know what that means, don't you?"

Vance nodded, already coming to his feet. He was looking in the direction of the sound and shortly saw two horsemen break out of the trees six or seven hundred yards away and below. Their horses were at a slow, slogging run as they climbed this way.

It was Hawks who said: "The one behind's Bill. And if the other isn't Ben Sayers, it's his twin. Well, friend, what now?"

Vance laid the bandanna against his side and quickly pushed in the tail of his shirt, drawling: "You walk from here on, Josh." And he stepped over to Josh's gray horse.

Josh's worried look deepened. "You're only beating your head against a wall, son," he said gently. "Now's the time to quit. Bill and me will keep the pack from jumping you."

"No. I'm still going to find Spane." Vance was in the saddle now, legs bent because the stirrups were too short.

"You're bleeding like a stuck hog."

"It'll stop."

Hawks sighed resignedly and, with a quick look at Bill and Sayers, said: "Then be on your way. Any idea where you'll be holed up?"

Vance nodded. "If I have to hole up, Josh, it'll be Bady's mine."

"How can you? The road's been gone for over three years."

Reining away, Vance said: "You can get in from above." He touched the gray with the spur and, as he started away, called back: "Lola Demmler told me about it."

Hawks slowly shook his head, watching Vance angle across the slope and then dip out of sight into the depression that lined obliquely downward toward the aspens. Then he turned deliberately, watching Sayers approach.

The lawman was red-faced and as winded as his horse when he pulled in alongside Hawks. His wary, excited glance went to the aspen grove and he snapped: "Vance, wasn't it?"

"Was it?"

Bill Childers came in on the other side of the wolfer as Sayers's angry glance swung down. For a moment it seemed the lawman was about to lose his weak hold on his temper. But then he gave a spare smile and, reaching to his thigh, lifted his

Colt out and aimed it skyward.

The three quick shots he fired wakened booming echoes that rolled along the dawn-lighted mountain. He holstered the weapon deliberately and looked at the dead brown up the slope.

"How did that happen?" he asked.

"Well, it was like this, Sheriff," Hawks said. "I was easing up here kind of slow when a big buck took out from the brush yonder. I made a grab for the rifle and it wouldn't come loose. First thing I knew I'd. . . ."

"You'd shot your nag through the chest," Sayers cut in dryly. "Those accidents happen, don't they, Hawks?"

"They sure do."

The lawman eyed Bill now. "You might as well get down and sit a while, Childers. We've got all day for this. There ought to be at least ten men here within the hour. Meantime, you two take it easy."

"Meaning we're under arrest, Ben?" Hawks asked.

"Not exactly. Let's say I'm just keeping an eye on you. In case of any more accidents."

The old wolfer shrugged. His sober glance came around to Bill and he slowly closed one eye, the eye away from Sayers.

Chapter Twenty-Two

Ames had come up Anderson's trail at 4:00, riding a little farther in this direction than need be before starting his climb into the higher hills. It was Tom who had suggested that he stop at the homestead.

Anderson's dog had wakened the family and the homesteader had come out. Once Anderson had the story, he went on in and told it to his wife while he was getting ready to go along with Ames, whispering so as not to waken Lola in the front room.

But Lola was awake and the men had hardly left the clearing before she put on her wrapper and went to the kitchen where Mildred had been fixing food for her husband to take along.

That was the beginning of one of the worst days Lola could remember.

There was no point in going back to bed, so she and Mildred had eaten then, both of them shocked over what had happened to Rita. As soon as it was light, Lola started on home. She was barely a quarter mile out on the trail when the faint echoes of rifle shots reached her out of the dawn stillness.

In her imagining she saw Vance being taken, wounded probably, perhaps dead. Or he might have made a getaway, in which case they were surely hunting him. She had never known such a feeling of impotence and dread as when, after listening for several more minutes and hearing nothing, she started on.

Later, after she had spent a sober interval wondering about Tom's part in all this, she was mercifully spared hearing Sayers's signal shots, though her worry could scarcely have been greater. For she was remembering what Tom had said after his meeting with Spane there at the corral the other night, and slowly the conviction was coming to her that Jeff Spane had neither the cunning nor the courage to have done this thing on his own.

Tom was the only one who, having seen this sure way of clubbing Jim Kirby into submission, would dare run the risk of carrying it through. It was impossible to believe that Fred Vance had patched up his differences with Spane to the point of working with the man. No, Tom must surely be the guilty one. He had been involved with Spane; he was still involved with him. As she faced this certainty, she saw all her hard-bought security of the past year falling away. Only recently had she felt that people were forgiving her for her divorce, accepting her again. And now Tom's treachery threatened to wipe out all the fruits of her humility and sacrifice, for if it was discovered she would be condemned along with him.

She couldn't fathom her brother's motives beyond sensing that his legacy of hatred toward the big outfits must surely be driving him. Knowing his weak and opportunist ways, she also sensed that it was characteristic of him to be taking this advantage of Jim Kirby and at the same time be serious in his intentions toward Rita. Had Tom shown her the signed deed for The Springs range, along with the statement Fred Vance had written on it, she would have known immediately that he was making a strong bid for Stirrup, that he had completely lost his integrity, but he had carefully avoided letting her see the deed for this very reason. So, though she halfway grasped the enormity of his deception, she saw it as simply a foolhardy and spiteful undertaking that was gaining him nothing but a shabby revenge at great risk.

She rode down on the cabin just past 7:00 a.m. and, as her apprehension grew stronger, she spent the next several hours at her housework, knowing that to keep busy was the only possible way of taking her mind from her troubles. She mixed a batch of bread and set it to rise; she aired the bedding and shook out all the rugs; she rearranged the shelves in the kitchen cupboard. Then, because the house finally became unbearable with its constant reminders of Tom, she took some twine and a knife and went to the foot of the yard path and began pruning and tying in place the thorny tangle of the rose trellis. That was where Sidney Connover found her when he came out the lower trail and along the small meadow shortly past midday.

She saw that Sidney's face was set in its usual soberness as he rode up and reined in just short of her. He touched his hat then in his typically polite way, saying: "Tom sent me with word for you, Lola. He thought you ought to know."

She felt a sudden constriction in her throat that wouldn't let her speak and her wild imagining pictured a number of dread things that might have happened. Her look must have been transparent, for he was quick to add: "Nothing's happened except that Sayers himself has seen Vance 'way up to the north. Vance was with Hawks and Childers. He had somehow lost his horse. He got away on Hawk's jughead and now I'm on the way in to get a telegram off to Sheriff Robbins across in Granite. Sayers wants him to bring some men across the county line and work in from the far side of the hills." He paused briefly, adding: "Then there's this business about Tom."

"What about Tom?" Lola's voice was hushed with fear.

"He was too far away to hear the shots when Sayers rushed Vance. Then when he did show up, he and Sayers had a real set-to. Worse than the one last night at the courthouse."

"Why, Sidney?"

"Tom's sticking up for Vance, claims he would never have done this. He even admitted to riding up Squaw last night and warning Vance of what was coming."

"Good," Lola breathed, a sudden forlorn hope in her that she had misjudged Tom. But then she knew that this would be his way, pretending loyalty toward Fred when he felt none at all. She tried to smile convincingly as she said: "It was good of you to go to the trouble of bringing me word, Sidney."

His glance was fixed gravely on her. "You think a great deal of Fred Vance, don't you, Lola?"

"Yes. A great deal."

"You don't believe he had anything to do with Rita's disappearance?"

"No."

"I had hoped. . . ." He caught himself and tried not to appear ill at ease as he went on. "Tom wanted me to tell you not to worry. He thinks Vance can find a place to hole up till they've found Rita. Fact is, he seemed to have a definite place in mind. Asked me to tell you that it's a place only you and he know about."

Bady's! she thought instantly, trying to hide her awareness of Tom's meaning by innocently asking: "I wonder what he was thinking of?"

"I wonder." Sidney smiled meagerly. "Ben Sayers would skin me alive if he knew I told you this. He isn't letting Tom work with the others, nor Hawks or Childers. Just as I left he had asked Tom to go on out and find Kirby, give him the word that Vance had been seen."

"And I suppose the senator is offering a really big reward this time for Fred?" Lola asked dryly.

Sidney shook his head seriously. "No. This has knocked the wind out of Kirby. All he wants is to get Rita back. He's got every man on his crew over there at Stirrup, pushing his cattle out." He touched his hat once more and, reining his horse on around, said: "I'd better be on my way."

"Good bye, Sidney. And thank you."

His—"See you soon, Lola."—as he was going away seemed a hollow promise. She stood watching until he had ridden out of sight into the pines, idly wondering what it was he had left unsaid a moment ago, halfway knowing what it might have been and wishing she had said something to bolster his unworded hope. She was fond of Sidney Connover but was too honest to deceive him in any way.

She forgot him then as her thoughts turned to the possibility of Fred's being at Bady's. And gradually a slender ray of hope shone through the gloom of her despair. If she could only see Fred and talk to him, he might perhaps make bearable the burden of her thoughts. Sidney had said that the posse was far to the north, which meant that it was unlikely anyone would see her riding that high country. She supposed that it would take her three or four hours to get up to the mine. But she was going. She was going now.

She was running as she went up the path to the cabin.

CHAPTER TWENTY-THREE

It was midafternoon when Vance glimpsed two riders less than a quarter mile below him. They had topped a rise and were slowly working their way along a hill fold he had traveled earlier. He knew then that he would have to be on the move and, favoring his right side, he swung stiffly to the saddle.

Over the next three hours he put Hawks's tough, hard-mouthed gray up to the timberline and there, keeping to the bare granite of the boulder fields, he swung sharply south. By 5:00 the high alp of Sentinel Peak was close on his left and he was riding for the notch Lola and Tom had last fall traveled on the elk hunt.

Without knowing what he did, he would have turned back shortly after dropping into the notch, for to all appearances it was impassable. First he climbed around a thirty-foot-high rock-slide that seemingly blocked the way. The worst was a two-hundred-yard stretch of narrow bare rock ledge flanking a sheer drop into a deep cañon where dusk was already settling. Down there somewhere was the break in the road.

He led the gray along the ledge. Beyond, around a shoulder of the peak, he came to the broad, timbered bench with the rusty sheet-iron roof of Bady's shaft house, a dull red blob through the thin sprinkling of jack pine and aspen.

He was feeling the wetness along his side as he had this morning, which meant that the bullet gouge had pulled open again. So when he came to the first grassy open stretch along the bench, he eased wearily out of the saddle and dropped the reins. As the gray began feeding, he pressed his right arm against the pad of the bandanna and let his head drop to his knees, admitting for the first time that he was nearly played out. He realized that he must have lost a lot of blood, and, as he looked back over the day, he knew it was one of the hardest he had ever spent in the saddle. It had netted him exactly nothing. He had had to give up the hunt for Spane as the posse crowded him higher into the hills. Now it looked like he was here to stay, powerless to move until this thing was decided one way or another.

These were his bleak thoughts when suddenly a sound shuttled down to him from above, from the direction of the ledge. His head lifted, he looked around. What he saw made him reach for the handle of the Colt he had taken from Byars the other night. A rider was coming down off this near end of the ledge onto the bench. For a long moment Fred's frame was tense. He had lifted the Colt halfway clear of his belt when all at once he recognized that rider and sighed his relief.

It was Lola Demmler.

She saw him now and ran her horse down to him. She was smiling radiantly as she drew in close. He came to his feet, and then she saw the stain along his side and her face lost color.

"Fred," she breathed, "they didn't tell me you were hurt."

"Who didn't?"

She understood his concern at once, answering: "Tom got word to me. Don't worry, no one else knows you're here." She came aground and over to him, staring down at his side with a frightened look. "Let me see it, Fred."

"Nothing but a chunk of skin gone from my ribs." He pulled open the shirt.

He heard her catch her breath as she gingerly pulled the bandanna away, and at once she said: "Sit down. We're going to have to do something about that."

He watched her as she went to the horse and unlaced a pair of pouches from the saddle. She brought them across and kneeled beside him, giving him a brief and tender look that had so much of her heart in it that it shocked him and gave him an instant physical awareness of her.

"You can't travel far with this." She was taking a bottle of whiskey from one of the saddlebags, uncorking it, and pouring some of the liquid on a clean handkerchief.

"That'd worry me if I had anywhere to go," he told her.

She leaned very close to him now, her coppery hair lightly brushing against his face as she said: "Hold your breath. This will hurt." Then suddenly she pressed the moist handkerchief to his side.

The whiskey bit into the wound like salt, and, as he stiffened, she said: "Now tell me how it happened."

As he began talking, she worked at his side, washing the wound clean, finally pouring some of the whiskey on it. When he had finished speaking, she said: "So now you're here and can do nothing. Have you wondered what's to happen from now on?" She sat back on her heels, watching him in that same deeply interested way of a moment ago.

He shrugged, puzzled by the directness and the intimate quality of her glance. "There are times when a man can't see very far ahead, Lola."

"Have you been looking ahead at all since you came home?"

He didn't grasp her meaning. "You're saying I haven't?"

"I don't know, Fred. We're practically strangers. But I've often wondered what you hope to get out of all this . . . this wrangle with Kirby."

Her seriousness suited her well, he was thinking. Yet he didn't understand her strangely intimate manner, her wanting to probe at his thoughts, and he said defensively: "A man doesn't let another just step in and take what's his."

For a moment she weighed what he had said with no break in her sober manner. Then, with the faintest of smiles, she told him: "I can understand that. But there must be something else driving you. Is it a woman, Fred?"

"No. Should it be?"

"That's what usually drives a man." She moistened the handkerchief again and, pressing it to the wound, made a pad of his bandanna to cover it. Her touch was light and sure as she pushed the shirt inside his belt and sat back again. "If you keep it clean, it will heal."

A feeling of gratitude for what she had done was strong in him now and, realizing what her coming here meant, he said: "A man never knows who his real friends are. This means a lot to me, Lola."

"Does it?" Once again he was aware of a deep and surprising response in her. "Then if it does, you'll leave, Fred. You'll leave the country and not come back."

"Leave? Now, when they've put a brand on me that doesn't belong?"

"Yes," she said quietly. "Nothing's to be gained by your staying. Nothing. And you can lose everything . . . even your life."

Her gravity awed him and for a moment he had the disconcerting conviction that she was halfway right. When she went on, her voice held even a deeper tenderness and sadness. "You must have found a good life somewhere else or you wouldn't have stayed away so long. Go back to it, Fred. Go back before it's too late."

"There's nothing to go back to."

"Perhaps there could be something." She spoke very softly and there was an unmistakable longing in her eyes as she all at once asked: "Would there be if I went with you?"

He was too surprised to speak and for a long moment she

studied his expression. "You see, Fred, there's nothing left for me here. I made a mistake. People will never forget that. This time I wouldn't be making one. You are everything I have ever wanted, and more."

He was groping for words, for some way of telling her that he didn't share her feelings. And in that moment he was taking a strict accounting of his emotions, seeing Lola Demmler in all her attractiveness, and it came to him that in time he might feel as she did now.

He was about to speak when she shook her head. "Don't, Fred." She came to her knees then, and leaned closer to tell him. "Don't say it. And I understand. This is only a beginning. Perhaps someday I'll have the answer I want . . . now that you know."

She bent quickly forward and touched her lips to his and suddenly a wave of a desire swept through him and his arms came about her and he held her close, answering the hunger of her lips. But then abruptly she drew away, lowering her head, trembling before a gust of emotion as she breathed: "This is something I can remember. Always. I'm going now, Fred. Don't say anything. Don't even watch me go."

She rose slowly and turned away. She was in the saddle before she said matter-of-factly: "There's food there. And I'll try and come back tomorrow and let you know how things are."

His glance followed her all the way up the slope, until she had ridden out of sight around the shoulder of the mountain toward the ledge. For many moments he sat thinking of her, wondering what halter there had been on his emotions that had kept him from giving way to the strong pull of her physical attractiveness, her offering herself, until that moment when their lips had met. Even now his desire had left him and he could look back on the moment he had held her in his arms with only a slight stir of feeling.

Finally the answer came to him and the knowing brought on his worry again. He caught himself comparing Rita with Lola and dismissed the thought, knowing he had unconsciously made a choice and that in making it he was the loser. For Rita was not for him.

He got up with Lola's saddlebags slung over his good arm and sauntered on across to the horse, picking up the reins and leading the animal down through the trees toward the shaft house. His thinking was at dead center. He was tired. He wanted nothing so much as to lie down and sleep the clock around.

There was a good stand of grass between the trees and the long slanting heap of the muck dump. He staked the gray out there, carried the saddle out beyond the reach of the picket rope, and dropped it. He undid the thong of Hawks's bedroll and, with it slung over his shoulder, started up the weed-grown path that led to the single empty doorway of the shaft house. Knowing the high country and the likelihood of there being a shower sometime during the night, he was going to sleep under a roof.

He was twenty feet from the head of the path when a whisper of sound above him made him lift his glance. There, leaning in the doorway, stood Jeff Spane with a Colt in his hand.

The shock of surprise held Vance motionless, and over the next few seconds a cold and killing fury was building in him. Here before him stood the man who had laid hands on Rita, a mocking look in his eyes and an expression of gloating on his narrow, sallow face. Vance was fighting an almost overpowering impulse to run headlong at Spane, to get his hands on him and beat the life out of him.

"Now isn't this luck," Spane shortly drawled, coming on out to the head of the path and hefting the .45 in a spare, menacing gesture. "Keep those hands where they are, friend. And turn around."

Vance didn't move. "Where is she?" he asked tonelessly.

Spane's head tilted toward the empty doorway. "In there. And lonesome, too. She'll be glad for some company. Turn around, I said."

For a second Vance tried to think of a way out of this, of a move that would give him a chance at Spane. But he had no chance. Both his hands were lifted—one holding the saddlebags slung across his shoulder, the other steadying the bedroll—and his gun was at his belt; he was dead the instant he let go of the bedroll to draw.

So he deliberately turned his back on the small man and a moment later heard Spane's boots grating against the rubble of the path, closing in on him. The hard snout of the .45 came solidly against his spine and Spane's move of lifting the Colt from his belt was deft, fast. Then once again he heard Spane's step and shortly the rustler said: "OK, come on up."

Spane was waiting there to one side of the doorless opening, his back to a litter of refuse—broken timbers, some twisted lengths of rusty sheet iron fallen from the roof, broken machinery parts, and a pile of broken clay retorts and pieces of glass. Vance started toward him and he edged farther back, saying: "Straight on in. And stop when I sing out."

The inside of the building seemed gloomy and cavernous as Vance came even with the doorway and looked in. He could make out no detail except that close beyond was a broad heavy bench with the shadow of a big cable wheel hanging low over it.

He was stepping through the opening when his glance picked out a hip-high length of two-by-four leaning against the wall close to his right. He went on another step, and then suddenly wheeled to the right, letting saddlebags and bedroll go and snatching up the length of wood. Before his swing was completed he hurled the timber hard at the doorway, lunging on into the deeper shadows away from the slope.

The two-by-four banged solidly against the doorway and he heard it go skidding down the path. He was taking his second quick stride when suddenly he tripped over something solid and fell headlong against a wall.

Even as he rolled to his knees and surged erect, Spane's low laugh was sounding. "Stub your toe, Vance?" he asked smoothly, stepping into the doorway and looking squarely at Vance. "I should have warned you. There's a dead-end on that side." He tilted his head again, indicating the part of the building abutting the mountain. "Try it this way."

Vance was hunched over slightly, his side hurting as he came on past Spane and walked into the shadows beyond. He passed a high, timbered ore bin, able to see more detail now that his eyes were accustomed to the half light. He climbed a series of steps that flanked the muck-car rails and beyond that the shadows deepened almost to complete darkness until finally, close ahead, he made out a plank door set in the granite face of the mountainside. The twin lines of the rails went under the door, which was held fast by a sturdy hasp with a rail spike thrust through its ring. This was the entrance to the mine's tunnel and shaft.

"Take down the lantern and light it," Spane said from behind him.

Vance saw a lantern hanging from a peg to one side of the door and reached it down, levering open the chimney. As his hand went to shirt pocket for a match, he was trying to gauge how far behind him Spane must be standing, for he was going to wheel and throw the lantern.

But then suddenly there came the hammer click of Spane's gun and the man was saying: "No one can hear this thing now if I let it go, Vance. Don't try anything."

Those words eased the tightness from Vance's nerves and sobered him as nothing else had. For the first time then he completely grasped the full measure of the man's vicious and evil nature. There had been no mercy in him the other night when he gave Bill Childers that beating; he would kill at the slightest provocation now. He had nothing to lose.

So Vance lit the lantern, and as the wavering light drove back the shadows, Spane told him: "Open 'er up."

He set the lantern down, lifted the spike from the hasp, and pulled the door open.

Rita Kirby stood there looking out at him. She was tall and slender, utterly lovely with her expression of sheer surprise at sight of him. For a moment her deep brown eyes were puzzled, disbelieving. Then she glanced beyond at Spane, saw the gun, and understood. Her look took on a quality of radiant gladness. Suddenly the pent-up emotion overflowed the dam of her restraint, her eyes filled with tears and, choking back a sob, she came out and into Vance's arms.

It seemed very natural that he should draw her close and put a hand to her head pressed so tightly against his chest. Her hands gripped the front of his jumper as she tried to control her sobbing. He could feel her whole body trembling and knew she was hungering for the assurance of this physical contact with someone she knew and trusted to wipe out the nightmare of the long, tormented hours of being locked in darkness. He was humble in the face of her complete trust in him, and, as he felt the tension slowly going out of her, he realized that this was one of the rare moments of his life. It was as though she were completely his, returning the emotion stirring him so deeply.

Her head lifted now and there was a disconcerting warmth and tenderness in her tear-filled eyes as she softly told him: "This makes everything all right, Fred. Everything. Just this."

"Was it bad for you, Rita?" His glance lifted to Spane, the softness going from it.

"Only in the beginning. It was . . . was my fault, I guess. I tried to break away."

Spane's look had taken on a faint quality of alarm as she was speaking. But now his face once again set in its arrogant, evil cast as he said: "She fought like a damned cat. Sure, I had to rope her onto her hull to get her up here. I'll be just as glad to get rid of her as she will be to be rid of me." He nodded to the tunnel opening. "In you go, both of you."

Rita looked around at him. "What are you doing with us?"

"Locking you in there together. Maybe for the night, maybe not that long, depending on how fast they get up here to turn you loose."

" 'They'?" Vance asked. When Spane only smiled, he put another question. "You mean the man you're working with?"

Spane still only smiled and shortly Rita said: "He won't talk. At first he claimed you were the one, Fred. Every time he'd say that, I would tell him he lied. Then finally, when I kept on asking, he just wouldn't bother to answer."

Vance had been watching Spane closely. "So you're pulling out. For good?"

Spane nodded briefly. "For good."

"It won't be as easy for you as it was this morning." Vance took his arms from around Rita and stepped back, lifting a hand to his side. "Sayers has got thirty or forty men down there now."

A look of alarm crossed Rita's face as she saw Vance's motion and she said in a hushed voice: "You've been hurt! How, Fred?"

"Our friend here." He nodded to Spane, adding: "Two inches farther in and he'd have had what he wanted. As it is all his lead did was scrape a rib."

He noticed Spane's puzzled look even before Rita asked: "This morning, you say?"

"Yes. Just before sunup."

"But. . . ." She glanced quickly at Spane, then up at Vance

again. "That couldn't be, Fred. He was here with me. He let me walk up with him to change the ropes on the horses. It was just getting light."

As Vance was taking this in, realizing the significance of what she had said, Spane drawled dryly: "So there's one mark you don't chalk up against me, friend." Abruptly he motioned with the Colt to the tunnel mouth, eyeing Rita. "You first."

When she didn't move from his side, Vance touched her arm, looking down and nodding. As she stepped over and into the tunnel, he asked: "Do we get the lantern?"

"So you can burn your way out? Unh-uh." Again Spane hefted the Colt. "In you go, Vance."

Vance sauntered on over through the door and in beside Rita. Behind him, Spane said: "Keep moving." So he took Rita's arm and started deeper into the black maw of the tunnel.

He was waiting for Spane's move, and when it came every nerve in him drew taut. Spane's boots grated behind him and then the shaft of the lantern's light shining weakly along the tunnel suddenly narrowed.

Vance looked at Rita, then beyond her to see that the wall fell away there into a deep pocket. At the instant it became completely dark with the door's closing, he pushed her out of line toward the inset, saying quickly: "Get back. As far back as you can." He was wheeling around as he spoke.

He lunged toward the door, marking it by the slit of light showing beneath it between the rails. He heard the click of the hasp a split second before his shoulder hit the door with all the driving weight of his big frame behind it.

The door swung sharply open for two feet before it hit Spane. The man's grunt of pain was plainly audible as the door jammed a moment. Then suddenly the lantern clattered to the floor, guttering out. On the heel of that sound Vance caught another as some object thudded to the planks.

In the feeble light he plainly saw Byars's cedar-handled Colt skid across the floor beyond the door. Then the door suddenly swung farther back before his weight and he was going to his knees as Spane's shape moved into sight.

Spane took two quick strides away and all at once halted, spraddle-legged. Vance threw himself belly down against the planking as Spane's .45 arced up and shattered the momentary silence with the deafening concussion of three shots quick as thought. From somewhere deep in the tunnel came the vicious droning of a bullet glancing from rock. Instantly Spane was wheeling away at a run for the steps and the lower level of the building.

Vance lunged erect. A stride carried him to where the other gun lay. Fear clawed at him, a dread that Spane might fire again and hit Rita, and he lined the Colt and threw a shot down the alleyway alongside the ore bin where Spane had a moment ago disappeared. He followed his bullet at a run, hauling up short when he was down the steps and within sight of the doorway at the head of the path. He started in on it warily, slowly, the Colt cocked and lined.

All at once a stray sound shuttled in to him from outside. He moved on into the doorway to see Spane below the foot of the path, working in frantic haste to put the bridle on the gray. Even at this distance, a good fifty yards, Vance could see the naked fear written on the man's face.

Spane saw him then and dodged in behind the gray, pulling the animal sharply around. A moment later the horse broke into a run with Spane holding tightly to his mane and throwing a leg over his back. Spane somehow managed to pull himself astride and the next instant turned and lined his Colt.

His shot and Vance's came simultaneously in one prolonged thunderclap. His bullet slapped into the board siding of the building several feet out of line. But a moment after Vance's gun had bucked against his hand, he had seen Spane's spare body jerk convulsively.

Spane swayed off balance, but then, riding well out of range, he pulled himself erect and raked his heels along the gray's flanks. There was nothing for Vance to do but stand still, watching the gray run on out of sight into the trees that hid the end of the ledge trail.

He sighed wearily, helplessly, and turned to see Rita standing there in the doorway close behind him.

"Well, he's on the way out," he drawled impotently.

"Let him go, Fred," she said in a low voice. "You're here and that's all that matters now."

She came in beside him, laying a hand on his arm and looking out along the slope for a long moment. Then she lifted her glance to meet his and there was an expression of longing and thankfulness in her eyes as she murmured: "I've never been so afraid. I . . . I thought he had killed you."

Her look was so wholly yielding, so much for him alone, that for a moment the hunger to take her in his arms swayed him closer to her. But then he remembered she could never be his and drew back again.

A wondering look lighted her eyes as she caught his hesitation. All at once she lifted her hands to his face, her touch light and caressing. Then, gently, she drew his face down and kissed him fully on the mouth.

Chapter Twenty-Four

The early hours of the day had been an endless nightmare for Tom Demmler, beginning with the realization that his shots at Fred Vance had missed the mark. He had cut a wide, fast circle down out of that high country and, as Sidney Connover told Lola, managed to make a convincing story of having been along the upper cañon of the Squaw at the time of Sayers's encounter with Vance.

The sheriff and Tom had their wrangle there in front of four other posse men, slowing Sayers's efforts to get them out on Vance's trail. It had been such a convincing argument that, directly afterward, Josh Hawks had led Tom aside and taken him into his confidence, told him of Vance's mention of Bady's mine. That news jolted Tom in the same way his missed shots had earlier, for the chance that Vance might meet Spane threw his calculations far out of their delicate balance. All his luck today had been bad.

Afterward, when he left on the errand Sayers had given him of taking Jim Kirby the news of Vance, Tom's resentment toward Lola for having told Fred of Bady's crowded everything else from his mind for most of the long interval it took him to come down out of the hills. He was almost panicked over the possibility of Vance's going up there and running into Jeff Spane and Rita Kirby.

But finally he reasoned that was unlikely. Hadn't Hawks and Childers said that Vance was half crazy with worry over Rita?

Hadn't they said he was hunting Spane and wouldn't hole up unless the posse crowded him too closely? According to them he hadn't been badly hurt; he was able to ride. *Then why worry?* Tom asked himself, in the end convinced that with all this country to hide in Vance had at least the rest of this day and probably most of tomorrow before Sayers could hope to begin really closing in on him. And by tomorrow Spane would be gone and it wouldn't matter who showed up at the mine.

Sayers having put him on his own, not trusting him to work with the posse, seemed the one good turn his luck had taken today. For he was meeting Spane at the corral tonight shortly after dark, meeting him for the last time. Sayers had made that easy. Spane would be on his way out with the last of the Marolt money, or rather that was how they had planned it, though Tom had revised those plans somewhat. Now that he didn't have to account to Sayers for his whereabouts he could ride where he chose.

He thought he knew where he would find Jim Kirby and had been riding for Stirrup rather than Box. It was around midday when from the crest of a hill high along Stirrup's east boundary he sighted a dull gray blob in the distance and guessed it to be Box's chuck wagon.

It was. Joe Banks was the only man at the wagon when Tom rode in some twenty minutes later. The wrangler was taking four horses from the long line of the picket rope and, answering Tom's query, said: "The boss? You'll find him somewhere along the north fence workin' with Foster and a couple others. Today he's just one more man to keep on top of a fresh horse. Same as the cook. Lord, we been puttin' in hours! Since one this mornin'. Anything new, Demmler?"

Tom told him about Vance, and then went on across to the chuck wagon where he helped himself to a plate of cold beans and some jerky. An hour later, two miles to the north, he spotted a thin haze of dust and rode across to it to find Jim Kirby riding the drag alone behind twenty-five or thirty head of his Box-branded steers. Ed Foster and Red Durns were working the draws along the swings.

Kirby was barely civil in his greeting. He listened without a change of expression to the story of Sayers's encounter with Vance, walking his horse on behind his gather of bawling cattle with Tom close alongside.

"Who was it took the shots at him?" he wanted to know when Tom had finished. His look was bleak, made more so by a day's stubble of gray whiskers shadowing his craggy face.

"Hawks says it was Spane."

"They better watch that damned old coot!" Kirby said heatedly. "He's more than likely in with Vance on this." Tom said nothing, and shortly Kirby asked in a clipped voice: "You think it was Spane?"

Tom nodded. "Yes. I think Vance would kill Spane if he could find him."

"So you've really gone and stuck your neck out for Vance. Last night I figured you might change your mind. Does Sayers know?"

"Sure. That's why I'm down here instead of up there. Ben wants me out of the way."

Kirby digested this information over a long silence, once swinging hurriedly away to cut back a cow that tried to bolt toward a side draw. When he came in beside Tom again, he said: "First Rita, now you. What the hell kind of a spell does this Vance work on you people?" Before Tom could insert a word, Kirby half turned in the saddle to move an arm into the north, continuing heatedly: "You know what Ed and I found this morning? Cut wire. A lot of it, same as there is over west. That rain washed out most of the sign, but I'd say Vance has taken more cattle out this end than he tried to over my way."

Smiling thinly, Tom drawled: "Didn't he warn you?"

Kirby accepted this reminder with a strange lack of anger, staring soberly ahead. Tom sensed that he must be thinking of Rita. When the man next spoke he was sure of it, for Kirby said: "All I'm interested in is pulling out of this mess with a whole hide. Though I'd give every last dollar to my name to be looking at Vance over the barrel of this thing." And he slapped the stock of the carbine riding in its scabbard under his knee.

Tom nodded to the animals plodding on ahead of them. "Want me to stick around and give you a hand, Senator?"

"If you've nothing better to do," was Kirby's answer. So Tom went on ahead and began working with Durns and Foster, taking turns with them in riding the hill folds to either side, gathering in every Box animal they came across. By 3:00 p.m. they made a count of forty-one.

It was shortly afterward that Kirby hailed Tom and beckoned him on back to the drag again. He let Tom walk his horse beside him for all of two minutes before looking around abruptly to ask: "Tom, could you find Vance if you had to?"

"Find him?" Tom frowned. "Now, you mean?"

"Today. Now."

Tom considered this a long moment, finally asked: "Why?"

"You want to find Rita, don't you?"

"Sure. But she's not with Vance."

"I happen to think she is." When Tom only lifted his heavy shoulders, Kirby went on. "But never mind if she is or isn't. Spane said he was holding her till I'd pulled out of Stirrup, didn't he? All right, I'm pulling out. We moved upward of eighty head through the wire between one this morning and noon. There's close to fifty more here and the others ought to have as many in their gather. I'm keeping the men at it tonight. By dark tomorrow we'll have the layout cleared. So I've kept my end of the bargain, haven't I?"

"You have. But it's Spane you want to find, not Vance. And he doesn't give a damn about your pulling out of here. That was a stall."

Kirby's look was baffled and he said in an angry way: "All I asked you was could you find Vance if you had to."

"Maybe I can, maybe not. It'd be pure accident if I could."

"You'd know where to start looking, though." Tom tilted his head reluctantly, uneasy over the turn the conversation was taking as Kirby asked: "Then will you take me along and start looking?"

"And have you put a hole through him if we do find him?" Tom smiled wryly. "No."

Kirby's jaw set hard and, reaching down, he drew the carbine from its sheath and leaned down in the saddle to drop it into the grass. "That satisfy you?"

Tom thought about it, turning over in his mind a notion that had suddenly struck him. He was wondering just how far he could stretch his luck and it was Jeff Spane, not Fred Vance, he thought of now.

"Well, how about it?" Kirby asked.

All at once Tom made his decision and, glancing across at Kirby's waist, at the .45 riding along his thigh, held out his hand. Kirby was a second reading his meaning and then soberly drew the Colt and handed it across. "Where do we head for?" he asked. And now he had reined his horse to a stand. His look was eager, less bleak than it had been at any time these past fours hours.

"I'm not at all sure," Tom told him. "But we'll give Bady's a try."

"Bady's? Hell, man, you can't get to it!"

Tom smiled meagerly. "Lola and I got to it last November."

"How? The road's gone. A man would risk breaking his neck walking up across that shale."

"He would. But he'd risk damn' little coming in from above. Which is how Lola and I got there."

Kirby's eyes had opened wider. Now, swinging his horse on around, he glanced out toward the westward dipping sun and said crisply: "We've got to move if we want to make it before dark."

CHAPTER TWENTY-FIVE

Had a man been able to scale Sentinel Peak, and had he known what to look for, he would have seen the line Jeff Spane was riding converging with the one Tom and Jim Kirby were taking as certainly as though the meeting between the three had been prearranged. Tom was playing a fairly sure bet. There was one way down off the heights of Sentinel in the direction Spane would be heading, one way only unless a man wanted to ride miles out of the way to the north. And Tom guessed that Spane wouldn't be doing much straying. The direct way led down an unnamed cañon, crossed a bench heavily timbered, and dropped from that spruce-fringed rim straight down to Cross D.

Tom had guessed wrong on one thing, the time of day Spane would be doing his traveling. It had been his hope that he and Kirby would meet the rustler on the way out of the notch about sundown. As it was, they were well back along the bench and riding through a thin stand of aspen for the wide mouth of the long cañon falling off the shoulder of Sentinel when suddenly Kirby, peering ahead, asked: "Who's that?"

Tom's head jerked up. He had been deep in thought. Following Kirby's glance through the trees and up along the wide rocky bed of the cañon he couldn't see anything at first and asked: "Where?"

"There. In behind that oak brush this side of that black ledge. Whoever he is, he doesn't have a saddle."

Kirby had reined in and Tom, stopping his animal, a moment

later saw a man on a gray horse ride from behind a thick clump
of brush six or seven hundred yards above. At that distance the
rider was hard to make out, but the way his legs hung so loosely
around the barrel of the gray told him that Kirby had been
right, the man was bareback.

That spare shape could belong to no one but Jeff Spane, Tom
decided, and with his pulse suddenly pounding so hard as to
make his words thick-tongued he said: "It's our man."

"Can't be Vance! Not big enough."

"No. It's Spane."

Kirby's glance whipped around. There was a wild light in his
eyes as he held out a hand, snapping: "Our bargain was only for
Vance." Tom at once understood and drew Kirby's .45 from his
belt and offered it. "No, the rifle!" Kirby said quickly.

Lifting his carbine from its scabbard, Tom was trying to hide
the vast relief that was coming over him. Kirby was taking
everything out of his hands, settling this in a way that would
call for no explanations, no curiosity on anyone's part. He was
saving Tom the exceedingly risky chore of killing the one man
who could betray him.

"God, if only Rita was with him," Tom breathed now.

"Don't think about that," Kirby said in a low voice brittle
with excitement. He was glancing off through the trees and
nodding toward a thick stand of aspen along a slope to his left.
"You get yourself out of sight off there. In case he doesn't come
straight on out." And with a quick look in Spane's direction he
turned and rode back deeper into the timber, the carbine in his
hand.

Tom watched until Kirby was out of sight and then, his eye
on Spane, walked his horse on up through the gray-bark aspens
a good hundred yards. He stopped there, looking back through
the trees, trying to spot Kirby and unable to locate him.

Glancing on toward the mountain once more, he stiffened.

For Spane, now riding from the mouth of the broad defile, was angling this way rather than in Kirby's direction. Moreover, now that he was closer, Tom caught the lop-sided way he sat the gray, hunched over and his right hand pressed to left shoulder. Once, when the gray changed stride, climbing over some rock, Spane swayed precariously and his hand came down and clutched the gray's mane. Tom briefly glimpsed a stain at Spane's shoulder and instantly understood that the man was wounded. Spane was less than a hundred yards away now, sometimes plainly within sight as he rode out of line with individual trees.

In those next seconds Tom had a decision to make. It was now obvious that Spane, if he continued on his present course, would go on out across the bench without Kirby having a chance at him—unless Kirby moved in toward him, in which case Spane would probably hear and make a break, taking advantage of the heavier timber farther out. But he was going to ride within fifty yards of where Tom now waited.

His decision made, Tom turned the bay so that his right side was away from Spane. He slowly drew his Colt and let it hang in his hand. Then, when Spane was almost abreast of him, he put his horse out from the trees at a walk toward the man.

Spane heard the snapping of a dead branch under the bay's hoof and suddenly straightened from his crippled, hunched-over position. His sickly gray face swung Tom's way. He saw who it was and the strident alarm etched on his drawn, pain-wracked features eased away.

He was even smiling as he turned toward Tom. And now the front of his shirt showed crimson from shoulder to waist. He sat unsteadily on the gray's back. Yet the sight of Tom seemed to give him new strength and he called: "God, do you look good! Vance put a. . . ."

The lift of Tom's right hand chopped off his words. Stark terror was in his eyes as his good hand made a frantic, wild stab at the gun riding along his thigh.

Kirby, watching all this from two hundred yards away, and not at all understanding Spane's strange behavior, saw the rustler's spare frame pounded backward by the roaring blast of Tom's first shot. Spane had managed somehow to lift his gun clear when Tom's second and third bullets drove into his chest. The gray wheeled sharply then, and Spane, already dead, fell loosely to the ground as his animal lunged away at a run.

For a long moment Kirby sat awed by the utter viciousness and brutality of the thing he had witnessed. Hating Spane as he did, he was nevertheless dumbfounded at seeing the man, already crippled, killed in such cold blood. He sensed something obscure and underhand in what Tom had done, and, as he started across, thrusting the Winchester into the scabbard, he was almost physically sick.

Some of this feeling of revulsion must have betrayed itself in his look as he rode in on Tom and drew rein, looking down at Spane's loosely sprawled body, for Tom said lamely: "You saw him reach for his iron."

"So I did."

Kirby's glance lifted now. It was so chilled, so probing, that Tom finally looked away, asking querulously: "Now what's wrong?"

"Nothing." Kirby spoke quietly, his glance still boring in on Tom. "Nothing at all."

"He's changed his last brand, made his last shady deal." Tom was trying to sound bitter, angry, but he sensed that his tone lacked conviction and he added: "He was dead the minute he touched Rita."

Kirby said quietly: "We can't just let him lie here. You pack him on down to your place. I'll keep on and see what luck I have."

"Finding Rita? You won't know where to go if you want to have a look at Bady's."

"You can tell me, can't you?"

Tom was about to protest Kirby's decision, but saw that he could give no logical reason for not doing exactly as Kirby suggested. So, briefly and in much the same way as he had described it to Spane the night before last, he told the senator how to get in through the notch and travel the ledge trail to the mine.

Kirby gave him no word of thanks, ventured no opinion when he finally turned and rode away, headed for the cañon mouth. Tom, watching him go, knew that never again would Jim Kirby look upon him as an honest man.

CHAPTER TWENTY-SIX

It was twenty minutes after Spane's headlong flight out along the bench that Rita and Vance rode the same way, Vance using Josh Hawks's saddle on Spane's claybank horse that had been staked out with Rita's animal in the timber above. The sun hung low in the west and the hush of late afternoon suited their mood. They were silent as they picked their way up onto the ledge and began traveling it.

When Rita finally did speak, Vance sensed that it was only to ease the awkwardness between them. "Spane made me take the lead when we came in along here," she said with a nervous laugh. "He was afraid I'd spook his horse on over the ledge. I had really thought of trying it."

"Wouldn't be much left of a man if he took that drop."

Vance spoke casually, his thoughts on something else. He was pondering that rare moment by the shaft house door that had shaken them both so deeply, blaming himself for having given way to his hunger for this girl. Her response still awed him when he thought back upon it, so complete had been her surrender as she melted into his arms.

No word had been spoken as they drew away from each other. Yet her eyes had brightly mirrored a blissful ecstasy as she had taken his hand and started on up through the trees toward the horses. He would never forget that in this moment the one woman he had ever loved had responded in a way that matched the turbulence of his own emotion.

Presently they reached the head of the ledge and rode on into the twilight of the notch where the high walls blocked out day's last strong sunlight, and as they started the climb around the rockslide—slogging, muscle-straining work for their animals—Vance was eyeing the future with a bleakness he had never thought was in him. Even though this trouble would finally be over with, life on Stirrup would be pointless, barren. He might somehow manage to keep from seeing Rita except on rare occasions, but the very fact of her being so close and possessed by another man would be a constant, unbearable torment. He would have to leave, go back to New Mexico, or anywhere that would put distance between them. It was senseless to think that he would ever forget her, but at least time and distance would dull the sharp edge of the bitterness and loneliness that was being born in him now.

At the head of the notch they angled on around the face of the peak and presently dropped down along the snaking course of a cañon, the brassy disc of the sun now shining directly in their faces as it topped the jagged western horizon.

The rolling blasts of Tom Demmler's three shots echoed up to them when they were perhaps a mile down along the cañon's depths and Rita turned to Vance then with a silent, faintly alarmed question in her eyes.

"A signal of some kind," he told her. "Probably Sayers. Like this morning after he had his look at me."

She merely nodded at his comment and the few glimpses he had of her face as they rode close together showed him an indrawn, thoughtful expression. He wondered at this but was too deep in his own thoughts to try to account for it.

It was perhaps a quarter hour after the sound of the shots when abruptly she broke the long silence, saying: "Fred, I need your help. It's about Tom."

He was immediately wary and only nodded, not trusting

212

himself to say anything. She sensed his uneasiness and understood it, eyeing him soberly to say with a surprising straightforwardness: "You were thinking of Tom back there. So was I. But it . . . it would have happened to us regardless of this other, Fred." She reached out and laid a hand on his arm. "Try to believe that."

"Regardless of what other?" was all he could think of to say as her words jolted him.

The toneless quality edging his voice made her draw her hand away. For several seconds she was silent, then, when she did speak, it was to say miserably: "I don't know how to tell it. All my thinking is so tangled. Now I know how Bill Childers must have felt that night after you'd brought him home. Nothing he had believed in made much sense. Now it's that way when I think of Tom."

"Why should it be?"

She caught that uncompromising, faintly angry edge to his voice and, because it meant so much that he should understand, she said deliberately: "It began that morning you and Bill took those shots at Dad and the crew. I was on my way across to see Tom and Lola when I came on Tom and Jeff Spane, talking up in the timber along the trail. They hadn't seen me, so I rode around them. I thought it would embarrass Tom to have me just ride up on them. Then later he denied having seen Spane. I. . . ." She gave Fred a helpless, pleading look, adding: "I couldn't understand it. I still can't. But he lied to me, Fred. Why?"

He was about to protest her judgment of Tom in the same way he had to Hawks last night at the line shack. But then suddenly and irrevocably he understood that she couldn't be wrong about the man. Now he was remembering Spane's and Rita's denial of Spane's having been responsible for those shots at dawn this morning far to the north.

His thoughts went quickly back over the past several days,

understanding with a terrible and startling clarity certain things that had held no meaning for him until now. It was then that Rita, misreading his silence, spoke again. "Don't think I haven't thought out what this means, Fred. I've tried my best to see it Tom's way. Of course he would hesitate admitting he ever had anything to do with a man like Spane. But if two people really care for each other, shouldn't they share confidences like that?" Vance only nodded, his thoughts too confused to let him speak. She went on: "Back there in the tunnel I took a good look at myself. I began wondering just how much I really cared for Tom. What I knew about his having seen Spane even got me to wondering if he could have had a part in all this." The way his glance came around to her now, alert and probing, made her ask: "Was that very wrong of me?"

"No," he replied levelly, checking any further words with the knowledge that the last thing he wanted was to say anything that would influence her now. "Go on," he added.

She lifted her shoulders and smiled faintly, guiltily. "This may be an awful thing to say. But it means everything to me that you should understand. There . . . there in the mine I finally could face the truth. Regardless of Tom's being honest or dishonest, of his working with Spane or not working with him, I know I don't love him. I never have. Admired him, yes. I've even pitied him and stuck up for him against Dad. But it's never really been love."

All at once now Vance's tiredness lightened. The bitterness and the hopelessness that had been in him were slowly draining away. He felt clean inside, buoyed up by a new hope he didn't quite dare recognize. He asked: "You're sure of this, Rita? Very sure?"

The look she gave him was grave, tender. "Yes, Fred. Very."

"Because there's not going to be any turning back from what's coming."

"And what is coming?" Her voice was hushed, afraid.

At that moment, as he was about to tell her of the things he knew now and hadn't five minutes ago, they both caught a sound shuttling up from below along the cañon. Vance, his hopes and longings alive once more, looked on down the high-walled corridor to see big Jim Kirby, riding toward them from around a high rock shoulder some two hundred yards below.

He said soberly: "Your father. You'd better go on and meet him. I'll wait here." And he reined in.

Rita glanced around at him, her heart in her eyes now. "I think I know what you were going to say," she murmured. "It's about Tom, isn't it?"

He nodded

"He was the man working with Spane, wasn't he?"

Again Vance nodded.

Rita turned away then. And before she lifted rein to send her horse on away from him, she said very softly: "It's between you and Tom now, isn't it? I will be waiting for you, Fred."

As she rode on, a strong tide of sober happiness rushed in to submerge every other emotion in Fred Vance's being.

CHAPTER TWENTY-SEVEN

The deepening twilight seemed to bring with it a strengthening gloom over Tom Demmler's thoughts. He would never forget his meeting with Lola there at the wagon shed as he was unroping Spane's body from the gray's back.

She had surprised him—before leading the gray down he had gone to the cabin and found it empty—by suddenly riding in out of the trees behind the barn. There was no time to get the gray and its grisly burden in out of sight even though it was almost dark. She had seen him and ridden quickly over, saying excitedly: "Tom, I've found Fred and you'll. . . ."

She had seen the body then and choked off her words with a small cry of alarm. Then, silently, she put her horse in closer to the gray. She recognized Spane and fixed on Tom a wide-eyed look of disbelief. "You . . . you did this?"

"Who else?"

"And where's Rita?"

Tom shook his head. "She wasn't with him. Kirby's gone to look for her."

A strange change came to her then. Her eyes were all at once alight with hate and she breathed in a tone of utter contempt: "You needn't tell me how it happened. I know. You murdered him. You're lost now, Tom. Absolutely lost! I . . . I'm leaving you. For good."

She turned her animal out from him, and, as a sudden rage struck him, he reached out and snatched at her reins, drawling:

"Not till you tell me what you mean! Why lost?"

Instead of answering, she lashed out with the rein ends, striking at his face so that he instinctively let go his hold and lifted his hands. She touched her animal with the spurs then and rode on out of his reach, straight up across the yard to the porch. A strange paralysis held him where he was, cautioning him against following her. He knew without being told what she must be thinking, that she had jumped to her own conclusions at sight of Spane's body, that she had her answers to the many questions she must have asked herself over the past several days. And he had no wish to face her now and hear how closely she might have come to guessing the truth about him.

He was undecided as to what to do now, whether to finish unroping Spane's body and leave it here in the wagon shed until Kirby arrived to take it on in to town. It was the thought of Kirby's possibly finding Rita and bringing her down here that finally decided him, and he unknotted the rope and went ahead with his work.

Spane's body was already stiffening and made an awkward load as he lifted it down and carried it in through the dark maw of the wagon shed. He found some potato sacks in the feed bin and waited until he had covered the body with them before going over to grope in the dark, trying to find the lantern that should be hanging from one of the harness nails.

He had barely lit the lantern when he caught soft hoof falls sounding up from the direction of the corral. He decided that it was more than one horse, and as the thought struck him—*He's found her!*—he stepped over to the door and outside, the lantern in his hand.

The shapes of two riders came slowly in out of the darkness toward him. Jim Kirby was in the lead, Rita following him closely. Then, as he smiled broadly and was about to call out, he made out another indistinct shape behind Rita.

He saw Fred Vance come on into the light astride Spane's claybank. In pure surprise he breathed: "Good Lord, all of you." Then he found the presence of mind to play out his part, adding: "Rita, are you all right?"

He didn't begin to understand what happened, the way Rita glanced down at him so aloofly, the stern set of Jim Kirby's square face, the deliberateness of Vance's climbing from the saddle and stepping toward him. He set the lantern down and tried to keep down the panic building in him, laughing and saying uneasily: "You're sure a sober bunch."

Kirby glanced around at Vance, asking tonelessly: "Do Rita and I stay, Fred?"

Vance only nodded, his glance not straying from Tom as he stepped several strides away. Then abruptly he was saying: "Tom, someone winged me up there in the hills to the north this morning. It wasn't Spane."

Tom felt the blood draining from his face. Yet now, when he needed it most, his nerve came back and he blandly asked: "Then who was it?"

"You, Tom."

Tom gave a visible start. And over the next several seconds he gauged his chances and found them slim. Vance's high frame was tensed, the fingers of his right hand clawed slightly as though he was ready to lift it to the gun thrust through his belt. Tom could sense the antagonism in Rita and Kirby, and, although he didn't know how much they had guessed, he sensed that this was one of the most dangerous moments he had ever lived through.

Now once again his courage strengthened unaccountably and let him put a slack expression of bewilderment on his face. "What? Me?" He laughed hollowly. "Friend, what are you saying?"

"In the beginning, it was Milt Hurd," Vance stated quietly.

"Because you knew he would never have signed your lease. Then you offered to hire Spane for me, probably because you were already in with him on something. Kirby says cattle have gone through that north fence. Maybe you could tell us how they. . . ."

"I can tell you, Fred!"

Lola's voice, speaking from the shadows, startled them all. Vance glanced briefly at her as she moved on into the light, then his eyes swiveled back to Tom again.

"Tom and Spane drove those cattle off Stirrup," Lola went on now, looking at Tom accusingly. She was pale and her expression was lifeless, burned out. "But none of the rest of the things you're saying are true. Tom may have stolen cattle, but he isn't a killer." Now her glance swung around to Vance. "Think, Fred," she said in a barely audible voice. "Think what you're saying! He's your friend. He's stuck with you when all the others have turned. . . ."

"No, Lola." Vance's quiet drawl cut across her words. "That's what I'd give anything to think. But it doesn't add up." His attention had strayed from Tom now. "Spane couldn't have thought of taking Rita. He didn't have the nerve for it. And you said yourself that you and Tom were probably the only ones who'd ever got to Bady's since the road went. . . ."

Tom lunged, the thin hold on his panic suddenly giving away, driving him to violence. At the limit of his vision Vance caught that move and swung around at the instant Tom kicked the lantern over and lunged away in the blackness.

Rita cried out as Vance was lifting hand to belt. For a fraction of a second that last glimpse he'd had of Tom hung in Vance's consciousness. He saw the man's solid frame bent over in that lunge, saw him drawing the gun at his thigh. In that instant he threw his body sharply sideways, his move barely begun before a rosy stab of flame was lancing at him out of the darkness in accompaniment to a blasting explosion. A regret surged through him as he lifted his gun, lined it, and squeezed the trigger. Over the throaty roar of the .45 he sensed that his bullet had gone home. He fired again, hearing Tom's hoarse scream as an after-echo of the concussion.

He took one more sideward step, and across the sudden stillness there sounded the hoarse rattle of Tom's breathing. Vance thought he could make out his friend's shape, then decided his eyes were deceiving him. But the next moment, when that shape slowly melted toward the ground and there came the dull pound of Tom's fall, he knew he wasn't mistaken.

A choked sob of Lola's finally broke that strained silence and Vance heard her run past him, indistinctly saw her kneel there beside her brother. He was turning away when she said softly, lifelessly: "He's gone."

Kirby, afoot now, struck a match and came walking over, and Vance was watching him go to his knees beside Lola, putting an arm about her shoulders, when all at once he sensed that Rita was close beside him.

Her hand nestled in the bend of his elbow, its pressure guiding him on away. They had taken several steps off into the darkness before he realized that he still gripped the Colt. He dropped it, and the thud of its falling seemed to strike a note of finality to this terrible moment. Rita stopped finally and stood closely in front of him, looking up at him. He said brokenly: "If . . . if only we'd been by ourselves, this. . . ."

She put a finger to his lips, softly saying: "It had to be, Fred. Do you remember telling me there was to be no turning back?" He nodded mutely and took her hand in his. Then, tenderly, she murmured: "So we won't turn back. We, Fred. Think what that means." And from the depths of his being there rose a humble thankfulness that thinned the sadness and regret and let him know that one day this dark hour would be forgotten.

ABOUT THE AUTHOR

Peter Dawson is the *nom de plume* used by Jonathan Hurff Glidden. He was born in Kewanee, Illinois, and was graduated from the University of Illinois with a degree in English literature. In his career as a Western writer he published sixteen Western novels and wrote over 120 Western short novels and short stories for the magazine market. From the beginning he was a dedicated craftsman who revised and polished his fiction until it shone as a fine gem. His Peter Dawson novels are noted for their adept plotting, interesting and well-developed characters, their authentically researched historical backgrounds, and his stylistic flair. During the Second World War, Glidden served with the U.S. Strategic and Tactical Air Force in the United Kingdom. Later in 1950 he served for a time as Assistant to Chief of Station in Germany. After the war, his novels were frequently serialized in *The Saturday Evening Post*. Peter Dawson titles such as *Royal Gorge* and *Ruler of the Range* are generally conceded to be among his best titles, although he was an extremely consistent writer, and virtually all his fiction has retained its classic stature among readers of all generations. One of Jon Glidden's finest techniques was his ability, after the fashion of Dickens and Tolstoy, to tell his stories via a series of dramatic vignettes which focus on a wide assortment of different characters, all tending to develop their own lives, situations, and predicaments, while at the same time propelling the general plot of the story toward a suspenseful conclusion. He was no less gifted as a master of the short novel and short story. *Dark Riders of Doom* (Five Star Westerns, 1996) was the first collection of his Western short novels and stories to be published. His next Five Star Western will be *Treasure Freight*.

9-13